Heart's  Secret

ADRIANNE BYRD

Heart's Secret

ARABESQUE®

Lad 9-1-12
Circ 6

HEART'S SECRET

ISBN-13: 978-0-373-83185-2

www.kimanipress.com

Printed in U.S.A.

Dear Reader,

We hope you enjoy *Heart's Secret,* the first book in Arabesque's MATCH MADE series. Over the next three months we will introduce you to The Platinum Society, an exclusive matchmaking service run by Melanie Harte—a third-generation matchmaker—for wealthy, high-profile clients.

Discretion is the better part of romance, or so Melanie Harte believes when she sets up the rich and handsome banker Jaxon Landon with Zora Campbell, a former model who runs a successful company. Melanie has promised Jaxon's grandmother that she will never reveal that she had a hand in getting Jaxon and Zora together. But can love last when it's based on a little white lie? Let's hope so.

In the months to come, look for *Heart's Choice* by Celeste O. Norfleet and *Heart's Reward* by Donna Hill to find out if The Platinum Society can help lovers find their soul mates and create matches made in heaven.

Evette Porter

Editor

Arabesque

Acknowledgments

To my dear and patient editor, Evette Porter.
Your encouragement and support are never ending.

Prologue

Sag Harbor, New York

"We're a *love* matchmaking service, not a *sex* matchmaking service, Mr. McElroy," Melanie Harte said testily into the phone. "I don't care if you have the fifty-thousand-dollar fee. I run a respectable and lawful business here. I'm not interested in becoming your pimp."

Click.

Melanie jerked the phone from her ear. "How do you like that? Bastard hung up on me." She placed the handset back into the cradle only to have it to immediately start ringing again. Exasperated, she glanced around the office. "Where in the hell is everybody?"

Riiingg.

"Good morning. Thank you for calling the Platinum Society. How can I help you?" Melanie Harte reached across her desk and picked up a gold pen, ready to jot down a message when she recognized the voice on the other end of the phone. "Ah, Mrs. Landon. How are you today?"

Outside Melanie's home office, a low buzz of chattering voices pulled her attention away from the caller. She looked up, just in time to see her two beautiful nieces, Jessica and Veronica, laughing as they strolled into the office. Five minutes late.

"Morning," they singsonged with bright smiles.

Melanie tapped her watch, but then her gaze shifted to the tall Starbucks coffees nestled in a cup holder. She started salivating as the coffee's distinct heady aroma kicked her caffeine addiction into gear. Melanie smiled.

"Here. Before you start drooling." Veronica chuckled, handing over one of the cups.

Melanie mouthed the words *thank you* and then accepted the warm cup of coffee. Not until after she'd taken the first sip did she remember that she still had Sylvia Landon chatting away in her right ear. "Uh, yes. Yes. I did receive your letter," she informed the spirited eighty-two-year-old. "I had planned on calling you later today since I was just about to go into a morning meeting with the staff. Can I call you in—say, one hour?" She took another sip of coffee and sighed at how quickly her foggy brain was clearing up. "Let me just get your number." She set the coffee down and quickly jotted Sylvia's number on a pink pad. "Great. I'll talk to you in an hour, Mrs. Landon."

"Now, you know better than that," the older woman reprimanded gently. "Call me *Sylvia*."

"Sylvia it is," Melanie agreed. "Call you back in an hour." She ended the call, and then hit a button to forward all incoming calls to voice mail.

"Sylvia Landon?" Jessica asked, surprised. "Not the one that's married to *Carlton* Landon?" she asked, ruffling through her tote bag.

"The one and only," Melanie affirmed and took another long satisfying gulp of her coffee. "God, I wish I could pipe this stuff through an IV."

"Who's Carlton Landon?" Veronica asked, her gaze bouncing between her cousin and aunt.

Jessica retrieved the latest copy of *Forbes* magazine and thrust it toward her cousin. On the cover, a picture of a stern-faced Carlton Landon stood with his arms crossed and the cover line The New King of the Mountain.

Veronica whistled. "Now *that's* an attractive older man."

"Yeah, tell me about it," Jessica said. "He's also loaded."

"Oh?"

"He's so rich he could buy five Oprahs, three Will Smiths and still have money left over for a couple of Shaquille O'Neals."

"Well, I ain't mad at him." Veronica laughed, still taking in the man's perfectly groomed silver hair, intense dark eyes and stone-chiseled features. "I ain't playin'. I'm really feeling this dude."

"Wait 'til you see his grandson," Melanie quipped and fanned herself with one hand. "Tall, caramel and handsome should be his first, second and last name."

Veronica's brows quirked up. "Caramel?"

"What can I say? Once they go black they don't go back."

"Hey!" Jessica held up her hand and gave her aunt a quick high five on that one.

Melanie added, "Sylvia Landon was also one of Grandma Harte's first love matches."

Jessica and Veronica's eyes widened with that information. "Really?" As usual the cousins gobbled up any and all news about their legendary match-making grandma.

"That couldn't have been an easy hook up back in those days," Veronica concluded.

"Yeah. It's been what—almost sixty years?" Melanie calculated in her head. "She was the best. Of course, I'm sure Grandma Harte never thought that she would be launching a business."

"Business? You mean a family industry, don't you?" Jessica said. "Considering that we're the third- and fourth-generation millionaire matchmakers."

Melanie conceded the point. The first Melanie Harte, a beautiful and unconventional woman of her time, played Cupid for the rich and lonely long before it was considered cool…and certainly before anyone realized it was a lucrative endeavor. Plus, she did it all without today's modern technology and pricey Manhattan PR firms, Internet ads or an over-the-top reality show. Melanie Harte's success came simply by word of mouth. Not to mention she held an astonishing marriage rate of 97 percent.

The current Melanie Harte was hot on her trail with 95 percent.

"Let's have the meeting outside," Melanie said, gathering up her folders and notepad. "It's a beautiful morning."

"Sounds good," her nieces agreed.

The women moved through the immaculate and extravagant office to access the mansion's wraparound porch through the French doors. The salty air put an instant smile on Melanie's face. She loved being out here, drinking in the picture-perfect postcard view of pristine waters and sailboats moored in the harbor.

The generations-owned, three-storied mansion sat on two acres high on the harbor's bluff. It had been photographed and serialized in numerous magazines and often hailed as an architectural and landscaping marvel with eye-popping gables, fifteen-foot ceilings, sunlit rooms, a conservatory, dock and boat slips, manicured lawns and a path leading to the beach and dock.

Quite simply, it was a dream house.

Once they were settled into the patio chairs, Melanie took another glance at her watch. "It's past nine o'clock. Where's Vincent?"

"Here I am," Vincent announced, stepping out on the porch, coffee in hand. "Sorry I'm a little late. My wife was looking particularly sexy this morning so…well, you know how it is." He hit them with a wink and a cheesy grin.

"TMI." Veronica rolled her eyes and then shivered as if the thought of her brother having sex gave her the heebie jeebies.

"Amen," Melanie and Jessica said.

Unfazed, Vincent chuckled his way over to one of the vacant whitewashed wicker chairs and plopped down. "So what have I missed?" Even though his official title was office manager, Vincent dabbled into other areas of the business's operations. He kept the company's books in tip-top shape and he was even known to make a couple of love matches himself—probably just to prove that he had the touch, too.

Young Jessica acted as the company's concierge and Veronica showed a real knack for the business as an expert profiler. Melanie suspected that it was just a matter of time before Jessica started hounding her for the title of vice president—if such a title existed.

"All right. Let's get started," Melanie said, taking another sip of her coffee and then setting it aside.

"Melanie wheeled in a big one," Jessica informed Vincent.

"Oh?" Vincent's brows jumped. "Anyone I might know?"

"Actually, yes," Melanie informed him with a cocky smile. "Jaxon Landon."

Vincent whistled low. "You're kidding me." He glanced toward Veronica and Jessica as if suspecting they were all playing a joke on him. "Midas Touch Jaxon is looking to settle down?"

"Apparently." Melanie shook her head, hardly believing the news herself. "Unfortunately, Jaxon's grandparents aren't too thrilled about his choice."

On cue her small staff blinked at her in confusion.

Melanie opened the folder on her lap and pulled out a lavender envelope and removed the matching stationery. "Let me read you the letter I received from Jaxon's grandmother. It should explain everything." She coughed and cleared her throat.

"Dear Melanie,

"I desperately need your help. My grandson has finally lost his mind. Yesterday, he had the nerve to inform the family that he was getting married. MARRIED! Now I know that you're thinking that this should be exciting news, but let me tell you, dear, that it certainly is NOT! The young hussy that he wants to give our last name to is, of all things, a stripper! A STRIPPER! Trust me— my mother is rolling around, keening in her grave.

"You have to help me, Melanie. You're my last hope in setting this boy straight. After all, it was your grandmother who was responsible for helping me find the love of my life and I've heard through the grapevine that your company, the Platinum Society, is doing a phenomenal job in continuing your family business of professional matchmaking. That is why I'm turning to you now. I know that you can help me. I don't care how much it costs as long as the result is a nice, beautiful young lady with the proper upbringing and education. Someone who can calm my grandson's rebellious side. I won't lie to you. It won't be easy. Jaxon likes to do things the hard way or no way at all. Simply put, he's as stubborn as a mule—just like my husband.

"I sincerely hope that you will accept my solicitation. Again, I must stress that I am a desperate woman.

"P.S. If you do choose to help me, I must insist that you do so with discretion. Jaxon will absolutely hit the ceiling if he finds out that I'm sticking my nose into his business. But I trust that you'll keep my secret.

"With much love, Sylvia Landon."

Melanie Harte lifted her large brown eyes and smiled. "So what do you think?"

Jessica blew out a long steady breath. "Wow."

After that, the continuing silence had Melanie wrinkling her button nose. "Is there a problem?"

Veronica drew a deep breath and brushed small strands of her long black hair from her angular face. Part of being the company's expert profiler was vetting and screening the varied mix of millionaires who so often solicited their services. Veronica didn't like third-party matchmaking—hell, none of them did.

"Well?" Melanie pushed.

Veronica glanced over at her brother as if mentally asking him to jump in—and he obliged.

Vincent cleared his throat. "It's just that the man is already engaged. It doesn't seem right that his grandmother is asking us to help *break up* a relationship in order to manipulate him into another one."

Melanie inhaled a startled breath. "It's not manipulating."

His brows rose, while his full lips quirked up in amusement. "Oh? And what do you call it?"

Cornered, Melanie shrugged. "I'd say that we were simply presenting him with a few more options." She smiled at her own quick thinking.

"You're reaching, don't you think?" Veronica chuckled.

Instead of answering, Melanie glanced back down at the letter.

Jessica waded in. "Is it just because of Sylvia Landon's history with our company? Is that why you want to take this on?"

Melanie responded with sincere honesty. "Yes. Besides, I already talked to Grandma Melanie about this. She thinks it's a good idea. Not only did she introduce Sylvia to Carlton, but they are also lifelong friends."

"Humph!" Vincent shook his head. "I still don't like the idea of us breaking up a relationship."

"We're not going to hold a gun to the man's head." Melanie laughed. "If he's truly in love then he wouldn't be tempted by the woman we select for him."

"*If?*" Veronica asked. "You doubt he's in love, too?"

Melanie chewed on her bottom lip as she mulled the question. The truth of the matter was that she knew and adored Sylvia Landon and the charity work she had done for the city of New York. She also knew her rebellious grandson Jaxon Landon and she, along with probably half the female population of New York, found it hard to believe the philandering playboy was turning over a new leaf for blissful matrimony—with, of all things, a stripper.

"Let's just say that the jury is still out." Her gaze darted back around the table where doubt and skepticism were clearly reflected on the faces of her small crew. "C'mon. You know the rules. I won't do this unless we're all in agreement."

"But how are you going to set him up with someone without his knowledge—and keep his grandmother's secret?"

"I won't lie, it will be a challenge." Melanie's smile widened. "But you all know how I like a challenge—*and* a good secret."

Chapter 1

"Zora, when are you gonna stop teasin' and go out with a brotha?"

Zora Campbell looked up from her script and flashed Todd Brady a smile. Though her supermodel days were behind her, it was still a boost to her ego that men continued to go out of their way to try and impress her. "C'mon, Todd. You know the rules. I don't date men I work with."

"All right then. I quit," he said, shrugging his mountainous shoulders and then spreading his LL Cool J–looking luscious lips into a wide smile. "There. That solves everything."

"You can't quit. I need you." She poked out her bottom lip and fluttered her long lashes up at him.

Todd clutched a hand over his heart and sighed. "Ahhh. If only that was true."

Zora laughed at his silly antics. "It is true. You're the best PR man in the business. Without you I would've just been another washed-up supermodel being a guest judge on a reality show."

Todd's chest expanded with pride as he strolled confidently over to the vacant director's chair. "Don't be silly, Zora. You have the face of an angel and a body designed for sin. *You* will never be washed-up because you'll never go out of style."

She laughed and shook her head. "With you around, my ego will never be deflated." She returned her attention to the thin script.

"Surely you know that thing backward and forward by now. It's our tenth infomercial."

"I do. I just get nervous before going on," she admitted. "I'm always afraid that I'm going to forget something."

"Relax. The Zora skin-care line is flying off the shelves. As well as the hair care line, perfume and jewelry line. America can't get enough of you."

"We both know this industry is fickle. There's a thin line between can't get enough and 'Damn, girl. We're starting to get sick of you.' If you don't believe me then go ask J. Lo and Beyoncé."

"I would rather we ask Oprah and Tyra."

"They have their fair share of haters, too," Zora reminded him.

"Of course they do. You're nobody until somebody hates you."

"That's an interesting way of looking at it."

"In this biz, it's the only way to look at it." The familiar ring of his BlackBerry interrupted the conversation. "Excuse me for a moment." He held up a finger and then reached inside his tailored Armani jacket and pulled out his phone. "Talk to me."

Zora returned her attention to the ten-page script and didn't look up until Todd was gone and the makeup artist was rushing over.

"You're here early this morning, Ms. Campbell."

"I'm always early, Beatrice. Force of habit."

Beatrice beamed. "I didn't think that you'd remember my name. This is only my second time working with you."

"I also never forget a name." Zora's smile widened. She had impressed the young lady. Even that feat she counted as an accomplishment because she knew that most people expected her to be a certain way. Pretty but not too bright. It was far from the truth.

Zora came from a long line of accomplished academics. Her mother, Billie Campbell, was a Pulitzer prize–winning author and economist, and her father, Elliott, had been a Rhodes scholar. Zora was well on her way to following in their footsteps when she was *discovered* studying at an off-campus coffee shop. Deciding to sign with the Ford modeling agency had upset the family. Her parents didn't approve of the lifestyle associated with modeling. Admittedly at that time, Zora had been seduced by all the trappings of fame. Easy money, VIP treatment and the possibility of the world knowing her name.

Upon signing, Zora had experienced a meteoric rise to the top six months after her first magazine spread. She made outrageous money for just smiling and playing dress up. It was fun while it lasted. But like all things, there was some bitter with the sweet.

For all of Zora's book smarts, she wasn't and probably could never have been prepared for fame's dark side. There was the endless supply of drugs and alcohol at photo shoots and wild, over-the-top parties. She had seen other girls become addicts and fall victim to abusive relationships. Some managed to pull themselves together, some died and some were just plain lost.

After ten years in the biz, Zora took her bow and allowed the next generation of beauties to take the stage. She returned to college, collected her business degree and then readied herself for the next chapter in her life. Not until Todd Brady came along did she think that stage would still include her selling her face and name. Turns out there were millions of women who were dying to know her beauty secrets. So she packaged them into a jar, slapped her name on it and set it at a price point that even Walmart-going moms could afford, and the rest was multimillionaire history.

The assistant director popped his head into the room. "We're taping in ten minutes, Ms. Campbell."

"Thank you, Henry." Zora drew a deep breath and steadied her nerves. It didn't matter how many times she'd done this, she still got a little nervous being in front of a camera.

Beatrice finished working her makeup magic and gave Zora the last five minutes alone before she went out on set. However, thirty seconds in, there was a knock on the open door.

Zora glanced over her left shoulder and then laughed. "Well, I'll be damned."

Melanie Harte beamed from the doorway. "I want to go on record that you have to be the hardest chick to find in Manhattan."

"Apparently not too hard." Zora stood up from her chair and met Melanie halfway across the small room for a tight, heartfelt hug. "How have you been doing, girl?"

"Fine. Fine. Like you. Busy as ever." Melanie, a fashionista herself, rocked a cute off-white pantsuit and a sharp pixie cut. In the fifteen years Zora had known Melanie, the woman didn't look like she had aged a day. Zora had the stray thought that maybe Melanie should get into the business of selling *her* beauty secrets.

"I dropped by hoping I could take you to lunch."

"Today?" Zora blinked, trying to think what she had on her schedule. Most likely she was loaded down with meetings and appointments. Mainly because that was how it was every day.

"C'mon. Say yes. It's been months since we've gotten together and just girl-talked."

Henry reappeared in the doorway. "Two minutes, Ms. Campbell."

"I'll be right there." Zora glanced back down at her friend and felt the tug of playing hooky.

"Don't front. You know you want to," Melanie pressed.

"All right. All right." She glanced at her watch. "It's going to take about two hours to film this twenty-minute infomercial. I can call—"

"How about I wait here on the set?"

Zora blinked. "You want to wait?"

"Sure. Why not?"

Zora's eyes narrowed suspiciously. "What are you up to?"

"Huh? What? Nothing." She tried to cover with a bright smile, but it only made her look guilty.

"Ms. Campbell, we need you on set."

"I'm coming." She moved toward the door, but then stopped. "I'll go to lunch with you, Mel, but don't think I don't know you're up to something."

"Who? Me?" Melanie batted her long lashes at her friend.

"Please. You ought to know better. That's my

signature move." She wagged her finger. "You're definitely up to something."

Melanie pressed her lips together in order to remain mum.

Zora laughed. "All right. I'll go to lunch with you but whatever else you have in mind, my answer is *no*." Zora winked at her friend and rushed to the set.

Melanie stayed behind with a huge smile on her face. "We'll just see about that."

"You know you're going to hell for lying to that sweet old man," Kitty Ervin warned with a wave of her finger. She softened the admonishment with a smile. In the three years she had known Jaxon Landon she couldn't remember a time she could ever stay mad at the sexy multimillionaire. In fact, it was hard enough just to be in the same room without having the impulse to rip off his clothes and try to screw his brains out.

"Sweet old man?" Jaxon Landon chuckled as he sat down behind his office desk and pulled out his checkbook. "You can't possibly be talking about my grandfather."

"Of course I am," Kitty insisted, leaning a hip against his sturdy mahogany desk. "Despite your efforts to inform your family of my lucrative career choice, every five minutes, your grandmother was nothing but kind to me the entire time I was there."

"My grandmother, yes. Carlton—that's a horse

of another color." Jaxon's rich laughter filled the large office. At six foot four and caramel candy–coated, Jaxon Landon managed the impossible feat of being both pretty-boy fine and alpha-male rugged at the same time. He was always immaculately groomed from head to toe, and the way he walked exuded a certain wild and dangerous grace. And his voice! His voice alone had the power to weaken the strongest sistah's knees.

"Besides, old money is nothing if not civil. It's what is being said behind closed doors that really matters. Trust me. My grandmother is likely crying to everyone who'll listen that her mother is rolling around in her grave—no—rolling around, *keening* in her grave at the very thought of me marrying a stripper. I love her dearly, but she does tend to be overly dramatic from time to time." He laughed, shaking his head.

Kitty's back stiffened. She wasn't ashamed of her profession. It was the idea that someone thought it eliminated her from landing someone like Jaxon Landon. Just because he was the new "Prince of Wall Street" and was cloaked in money, power and respect didn't mean that he was out of her league. It just meant that she would have to step up her game.

Jaxon noticed that Kitty's playful smile had vanished. He lowered his gold pen and rose from his chair. Jaxon kept forgetting people—mainly women—tended to be thrown off by his bluntness. He smiled as he moved around the desk. When he placed his large hands on her small shoulders and started massaging, he could tell by her twinkling eyes that all had been forgiven. "Sorry, Kitty. But I warned you before you accepted the job not to take anything that happened personally. My family can be closed minded and cruel sometimes."

She laughed, and then spoke before thinking. "It's not your family you should be apologizing for."

Jaxon's hands stilled on her shoulders. "What do you mean?"

Kitty mentally kicked herself. "Nothing." She gently shrugged off his hands and moved from the desk. "My check?"

Jaxon couldn't let such a flippant comment go. "Are you saying you thought *I* was somehow being unreasonable?"

Kitty really didn't want to get into it. After all, it was none of her business whatever drama went on between him and his family. Chances were that she would never see them again anyway. Plus, she didn't want to piss off Jaxon to the point that he would stop coming to the Velvet Rope. The women that competed for his attention grew more fierce every time he showed up. As it was, she was already the envy of every dancer in the place. Mainly because she had the advantage of knowing that it took more than big breasts, a slim waist, onion booty and a pretty face to grab and hold his attention.

Jaxon was an unusual client when it came to his visits to the gentlemen's clubs. He wasn't there to zero in on certain body parts. No. He generally enjoyed the *art*. He was particularly fond of the burlesque style as opposed to straight grinding on a pole and booty poppin' in a sequined string thong.

Smiling, Kitty leaned forward and let her expensive breasts press against his chest. "I would never suggest that you were ever unreasonable," she assured, blowing her strawberry scented breath up at him. "You have to be the kindest, most generous man I know." And she meant it. Jaxon Landon was known for many things: a *son of a bitch* when it came to business, *dangerous* when it came to those who crossed him and a *heartbreaker* when it came to women who had the misfortune of falling in love with him.

But the one thing very few people knew about him was that he genuinely had a heart of gold when it came to people he cared about. It was no accident that she was the one to land the ten-thousand-dollar job to pretend to be his fiancée for the weekend. Kitty knew that word had gotten around the club about her grandmother's increasing medical bills.

Last week she was sobbing into her pillow, worried about where she was going to come up with an extra ten grand for her grandma's surgery and then the next thing she knew, Jaxon was on her doorstep with a job for the exact amount of money she needed. That day she swore she could see a halo encircling the man's head.

And now, she had just insulted him.

"Then what *are* you saying?" Jaxon asked, standing up straighter.

"Oh, you know," she said, trying to stall.

Jaxon's smile flatlined while he waited.

Cornered, Kitty licked her lips and tried to swallow the growing lump in her throat. Whenever Jaxon leveled his intense mahogany eyes on someone, it had all the potency of drinking a bottle of truth serum. "I just meant that you seemed more…tense when you're around your grandparents," she confessed. "Once or twice, you may have come off a little short." She shrugged and then tried laughing. "But, hey, I'm the same way around my folks. I don't understand them and they certainly don't understand me."

The office grew as silent as a tomb for two seconds. The longest two seconds of Kitty's life. It wasn't that she feared that Jaxon would suddenly erupt and fly off the handle. He would never do that. It wasn't his style. It was all about his expressions and body language. A flicker of disappointment from him had the same effect as a parent scolding a child and whenever his beautiful eyes narrowed it was like a dagger piercing a heart. And if his rich baritone dipped to a rumbling bass, you knew your ass was in serious trouble.

Then out of the blue, Jaxon's smile was back. His perfect pearly white teeth and full, luscious lips had a way of making her feel like Cupid's bow had pierced her heart. It was crazy how easily Jaxon could turn her on. It was like flicking on a light switch. More than anything, she wished that she meant more to him than just a plaything.

"You're right," Jaxon admitted, chuckling. "I do tend to get...worked up around Carlton." He pivoted and returned to his chair to finish writing her check.

"May I ask you something?" she ventured.

"Of course you can."

"Why do you call your grandfather *Carlton?*"

"It's his name, isn't it?" He finished his signature with a flurry and then pulled the single check from its leather-bound book. "Here you go, m'dear. Ten thousand dollars. Not bad for two days of putting up with my *unreasonable, short* temper." There, he got in his jab.

Just then, Jaxon's secretary, Janine, buzzed in over the intercom. "Mr. Landon, Richard Myers is here to see you."

What in hell could he possibly want? Jaxon rolled his eyes. "Send him in."

Kitty reached over and accepted the check.

"Thank you." She folded it several times and then stuffed it in between her huge tits. "It's been a pleasure. Call me again whenever you're in need of a fiancée." She gave him another quick smile and then headed toward the door. "So when will I see you again?"

"Just when you begin to miss me," he teased.

"I'll miss you as soon as I walk out of the door," she volleyed back at him.

"Then I guess I'll see you at the Velvet Rope tonight," he said.

Kitty's heart skipped a beat. "Is that a promise?"

Jaxon winked. "Absolutely."

She turned, opened the door and nearly smacked into Richard Myers.

"Well, hello there, Kitty," Richard greeted coolly. "I didn't know you did house calls."

Kitty smiled at Jaxon's number-one rival—in everything from looks, women and business. The man took competition to a whole new level and didn't care who knew it. Kitty didn't mind it so much, since it meant twice the haters and two rich, gorgeous men lavishing her with money and gifts.

"Really, Richard. You should get your mind out of the gutter," she teased playfully. "I'll see you tonight, Jaxon," she said, tossing him a final wink. The comment was for Richard as well as Jaxon and if her calculations were correct, she would be seeing Richard tonight at the club, too. "G'bye, you two."

She gave them a dainty wave and practically floated out of the office.

Richard stood at the door and watched Kitty's rear view until she disappeared from the office lobby. Then he turned his sly smile toward Jaxon. "She's quite a woman, isn't she?"

Instead of answering, Jaxon relaxed behind his desk. "So what brings you here, *Dick?*"

Richard's smile only stretched wider as he closed Jaxon's office door and casually strolled over to the bar. "Oh, I was in the neighborhood and thought that I would come by and congratulate you on the Culberson deal. It must have been an awfully reliable bird that told you that they were in talks with Microsoft."

Jaxon kept his face neutral while he mentally patted himself on the back for putting the pieces of a very large puzzle together on his own. "Oh, I don't know. I'd say it was just a lucky guess."

A smile slithered across Richard's face while he poured himself some of Jaxon's good brandy. "Let you tell it, you're the luckiest sonofbitch in New York."

"Maybe I am," he said, holding his straight face.

A muscle twitched just below Richard's right eye. A telltale sign of what the man was really thinking and feeling—which was also the reason Jaxon always beat the man at poker.

Some things were too easy.

"You want to know what I think?" Richard asked, taking his glass and making his way over to the empty chair in front of Jaxon's desk.

"The better question is, 'Do I care?'"

"I think," Richard went on, "that you have an inside track on what's going on."

Jaxon glared. "That's one helluva accusation."

Richard's devious smile stretched almost from ear to ear. "Come now. I'm not accusing you of anything...*yet.*" He sipped his drink. "Then again. It could be just like you said." He met Jaxon's stony gaze. "You're lucky."

The room thickened with a deadly tension, but the ever cool Jaxon waited out his adversary.

"Anyway, congratulations are in order." Richard drained the rest of his brandy and got back to his feet. "We all can't make ninety million in a day." He purposely set his empty glass on Jaxon's desk and headed back toward the door. "See you around, Jax."

"Sure thing, *Dick.*"

Richard only chuckled as he made his grand exit.

Jaxon waited until the door slammed closed before muttering under his breath. "I really hate that asshole."

Chapter 2

"Hell, no," Zora said, and then proceeded to laugh in Melanie's face. "What did you do, fall and bump your head?"

Melanie laughed, as well. "I know it may sound crazy…"

Zora cocked a brow. "It *may?*"

Melanie tried again. "Okay. It *is* crazy. But come on. Humor me. I've got a feeling about this."

"Oh. One of your *feelings.*" Zora made air quotes and a look that said Melanie had lost her damn mind. "No offense, Mel. But I'm not sure I even get what it is that you do. Rich men pay you to find them women. Isn't there another word for that? Starts and ends with a *P?*"

"You're not funny," Melanie said. "Why are you giving me grief about this? It's not like you're dating someone." She frowned. "Are you?"

"If I said yes, would you drop this ridiculous idea?"

"Probably after I ran a background check on the guy."

Zora laughed as she reached for her wineglass. "That would be funny if it weren't probably true."

"We'll never know since you never date."

Stunned, Zora set her glass back down. "What are you talking about? I date."

"Yeah. Every full moon." Melanie shook her head at such a waste. "And I don't get it. Everywhere you go men are asking you out, but you never accept."

Indignant, Zora sputtered, "That's not true."

"Excuse me, ladies," their waiter interrupted as he returned to their table with a new bottle of wine. He showed Zora the label.

"What's that? We didn't order more wine," Zora said.

The waiter smiled. "Yes, ma'am. The bottle is compliments of the gentleman over at the bar." He popped the cork.

Melanie's and Zora's gazes followed the direction their waiter indicated with the tilt of his head to where a tall, handsome brotha lifted his glass and winked. The women smiled their thanks and then glanced at one another.

"See?" Melanie said.

"Whoa. We don't know if the bottle was for me, you or both of us," Zora reasoned.

The waiter cut in. "Mr. Blackburn asked that I also give you this, Ms. Campbell." He held out the gold-embossed business card. "And to tell you that he enjoys your work."

Zora accepted the card while Melanie sat back with an I-told-you-so expression. "That doesn't count," Zora said. "Fans do things like that all the time. It's flattering but—" she shrugged "—they're more in love with an image. You know. You've been there."

Melanie had indeed been there. In her early twenties, she, too, had been on the fast track in the high-fashion world of modeling. In fact, she and Zora met and were roommates in a Manhattan apartment building that housed young models back in the day. Within minutes of meeting, the two women fell into an easy friendship that lasted over the years.

"Then in that case," Melanie continued, "you should trust me to find you someone that won't be intimidated by your money or fame."

"I don't know. This whole thing still has a pimp-ish feel to it."

Melanie rolled her eyes. *This isn't gonna be easy.*

The waiter poured the ladies two new glasses of wine and instructed them to "Enjoy."

They both flashed him a brief butterfly smile and then fell silent as Zora read and then reread the business card. Either she was contemplating calling the brotha or tossing the card like she normally did.

"Soooo." Melanie picked up her fork and stabbed a few vegetables in her salad. "Are you going to call him?"

"Yes," Zora decided, but then countered. "Maybe." She shrugged. "I don't know."

"See?" Melanie dropped her fork and shook her head. "Why do you do that? You always shut the door on opportunity."

"Please don't lecture. I didn't bring my bottle of Excedrin."

Melanie kept charging ahead. "A career is great, Zora. But it won't warm your bed at night."

Zora laughed. "You're a fine one to talk." She reached across the table and grabbed Melanie's right hand. "I don't see a ring on *your* finger, Ms. Millionaire Matchmaker. Don't you think you're being just a little hypocritical?"

"We're not talking about me," Melanie said, a bit more testily than she liked.

"Maybe we should talk about you." Zora wasn't going to relent now that she had an opening to get her dear, but nosy and pushy, friend off her back. "I mean…shouldn't you lead by example?"

"Hold up. That's not fair. I'm a widow," Melanie countered. "Or have you forgotten that?"

"Of course I haven't forgotten." Zora released her hand, but then chose her next words carefully and softly. "But Steven has been gone for quite a while."

Melanie reached for her wine. "It doesn't feel like it was all that long ago."

"I'm sorry," Zora said contritely. "I shouldn't have brought it up."

Melanie drew a deep breath and tried to force the memories back where they belonged—in the past. She needed to focus on the matter at hand and that was pulling off the miracle of getting Zora Campbell and Jaxon Landon together. For now she would have to chalk this day up as a loss. She had lost control of the conversation and she would have to approach the subject another time and in another way. But no worries. Melanie wasn't the type to give up so easily.

"So I hear you're getting married," Dale Forrester yelled above the Velvet Rope's pulsing hip-hop bass before he invited himself to plop down at Jaxon's private booth with his usual double Scotch sloshing in his left hand. "When I heard, I couldn't fuckin' believe it so I figured that I would come and get it straight from the horse's mouth."

Relaxed and dressed head to toe in casual, black Valentino, Jaxon favored his old friend and mentor with a lopsided grin. "Do you come bearing gifts?"

"Hell, no," he half slurred. "I came to beat some sense into you." Lately Dale's face seemed to be permanently flushed a deep burgundy. Either it was way too much booze or rising cholesterol. Jaxon didn't know which, so he constantly hounded his friend about both.

Each time, Dale just waved off any and all health concerns. He didn't like being preached to and only mildly tolerated it from Jaxon.

"Please tell me that it's nothing but a nasty rumor and then maybe I can get back to living my life vicariously through you—such as it was." He turned up his drink and drained the contents in one long gulp.

Amused, Jaxon took a swig of his own whiskey sour and cast a lazy glance toward the exotic dancer working the pole. She wore a bit too much makeup, but he could tell that she at least had some formal dance training.

"So what's the story?" Dale asked, pulling Jaxon's attention back from the stage. "Are you walking the single's man plank or what?"

Jaxon considered toying with the man, but there was such a desperate hope twinkling in his eyes that he just couldn't bring himself to do it. "Chill, old man. I'm not engaged."

A broad, goofy grin broke across Dale's face. "Sweetheart," he yelled out to a passing waitress and held up his empty glass. "Another round. Happy days are here again."

Jaxon laughed. It was what he did whenever he and Dale partied together. For all the man's talk of idolizing Jaxon and his Midas touch when it came to business, Jaxon knew it was more because Dale remembered a time when *he* was hailed as the Prince of Wall Street. Unfortunately, his reign was shorter than he'd liked and it all ended with him serving some jail time. For the most part, the friends avoided both subjects. However, Jaxon was determined to learn from his friend's mistakes and he made sure that all his dealings were aboveboard.

Given all the temptations of Wall Street, it was harder than it sounded.

"I shoulda known to have more faith in you." Dale winked, plopping a fat ice cube into his mouth and then chomping away as if he was munching on a handful of M&M's. "Take it from me, marriage is highly overrated and expensive to boot."

"Better not let Mrs. Forrester hear you talking like that."

"Trust me. I'm not telling you nothing she doesn't know or hear from me on a regular basis. Destiny married me for my money and she'll divorce me for my money one of these days. That or she'll kill me for it."

"You poor, miserable soul." Jaxon chuckled, and then cast another fleeting glance toward the stage in time to see Gemini do a classic V swing, stand, drop it real low and back her luscious behind toward the crowd of panting customers. Benjamins rained down onto the stage and Gemini continued working her hips like the rent was due in the morning.

"God bless her," Dale muttered under his breath and then wiped the side of his mouth for a drool check. "I swear that girl makes me want to put her momma on my Christmas list."

Jaxon suppressed a grin with another gulp of whiskey. He smiled when he finally felt his afternoon buzz kick in. In fact, all that was missing was a fat Cuban cigar and busty temptress to end another trying day.

"Your drinks, gentlemen." Honey flashed them each a radiant smile and then set their new drinks on the table before them.

Jaxon and Dale took the opportunity to appreciate their favorite waitress's large glitter-dusted breasts and caramel-capped nipples.

"Can I get you two anything else?" she asked, centering her twinkling gaze on Jaxon. "Anything at all?"

The corners of Jaxon's lips curved upward. "I think we're good."

"Speak for yourself," Dale countered gruffly and then smacked a crisp hundred-dollar bill on top of the table. "Junior and I are in the mood for a lap dance."

Jaxon didn't correct him because everyone—or rather all the regulars—knew Dale referred to his small dick as *Junior.* There was never any shame to his game, either. He laughed at small dick jokes and would crack a few himself. If there was any time that Jaxon grew uncomfortable with his friend's self-deprecating humor, it was when Dale kept talking about his dick as if it was a separate entity. Dale was always going with, "Junior was looking for a nice warm place to sleep for the night" or "Junior was just standing up to say hello" or "Junior and I was talking last night."

Jaxon used to find Dale and Junior's stories hilarious. Now, since a night didn't pass without Junior being mentioned, Jaxon worried whether Dale and Junior were getting a little too close. (If that made any sense.)

Despite the fact that Honey was supposed to be waitressing, she set her small tray down and instantly started rocking and swinging her hips in perfect time to Beyoncé's latest jam. One of Dale's silly grins slid into place as he watched the up close and personal action prance in front of him, tempting and seducing him to reach for his wallet again.

Jaxon split his attention between Gemini and Honey and realized that *he* held their attention, as well. Gemini took a deep bend at the waist, wiggled her gorgeous brown behind and tossed Jaxon a smile. To his right, Honey shimmied her gravity-defying tits in Dale's face while giving Jaxon the anytime-anyplace look.

Jaxon smoothly gave both women an appreciative smile that neither encouraged nor discouraged their pursuit. It was a gift. His mother used to brag endlessly about him being a born charmer. He couldn't remember a time when he didn't love or more importantly when women didn't love him. In his adolescent days he played doctor so much it was assumed that he would become one.

He didn't, but he still played one from time to time.

"Well, if it isn't my lovable fiancé," Kitty cooed as she sauntered over to the small table. For Honey's benefit, she lazily but very dramatically draped an arm around Jaxon's shoulders. "Glad to see that you could make it."

"Of course." Jaxon smiled. "You know I always keep my promises."

Kitty's smile broadened as she eased down onto his lap. "In that case, what do you say to you and me hooking up after the show?"

"I'd say I love to," he admitted, running a finger beneath her chin.

Kitty lit up like a Christmas tree.

"*But*—I can't. I'm flying out of the city tonight right after I watch your set."

Caught between disappointment and flattery, Kitty's smile faltered. There wouldn't be any point in complaining or pouting. That would be the fastest way to chase Jaxon Landon away. She had been playing her cards right all this time, she wasn't about to screw it up now.

"Well, I'm glad you made it tonight." She caught

sight of Bishop nodding his head, signaling for her to get ready for her number. The only problem was that she was all too comfortable leaning against Jaxon's firm muscled chest. Not only did he feel good, but he smelled divine.

Jaxon glanced at his Rolex. "Showtime."

Reluctantly, Kitty climbed out of his lap but then caught sight of Richard Myers coming in the door. The man was as predictable as the seasons. "Well, it looks like I have another fan tonight."

Jaxon followed Kitty's line of vision and felt his general good mood take a nosedive.

"Oh, cheer up. You could do with a little competition," Kitty said and sashayed her way backstage.

"Yeah. You *could* do with a little competition." Dale chuckled under his breath as he slid one last Benjamin between Honey's string thong at the end of her dance.

"Thank you, baby." She blew him an air kiss, but tossed a wink over her shoulder at Jaxon.

Dale caught the sly move and sighed. "Fifteen hundred dollars down the tube."

Jaxon grinned. "I don't know. It seems like you were enjoying it to me."

"My dick is hard if that's what you mean." Dale smirked. "But it doesn't mean that I'm going to get any tonight."

"I don't know." Jaxon shrugged. "You could always go home and screw your wife for once."

Dale laughed. "I might have a pocket full of Viagra, but that doesn't mean that I'm *that* desperate."

Jaxon's head rocked back with a rumbling laugh. "You're a complicated man, Dale. No doubt about that."

"Speaking of complicated, when the hell are you going to fill me in on this vicious rumor circulating around town?"

Jaxon's smile ballooned. "It's a long story."

"You're in luck. I like bedtime stories."

Jaxon shrugged and leaned forward. "Let's just say it's a little joke at my grandfather's expense. I took Kitty up to my grandparents' place this weekend. Figured I'd try to get them off my back about settling down by bringing a woman they would never approve of as my fiancée. I never knew a man could turn so many different shades of purple."

"Should've known." Dale's smirk stretched into a callous grin. "I hate to be the one to tell you this, but you and Carlton are two peas in a pod."

"Don't even joke about something like that."

"The truth is an inconvenient thing, my brotha. Inconvenient indeed."

"Hello, gentlemen," Richard said after finally making his way over to the table. "Mind if I grab a seat?"

"Knock yourself out," Jaxon said, determined to be unfazed by the intrusion.

But Richard had a sixth sense when he was gettin' under Jaxon's skin and he reveled in it as he took his seat.

As if to spare them from having any further conversation, the club's music changed and the main attraction got underway. Jaxon gladly turned his attention toward the stage. Kitty stretched out a long, curvy leg from behind a red curtain. Every man in the joint hooted and whistled their approval only for Kitty to pull the leg back as if she was suddenly too shy. The next time there was a little more leg, plus the curve of her hip. A very nice hip at that.

"The girl is a pro," Dale praised. "I'm getting so hard, I just might have to go home and screw my wife."

Jaxon laughed. "God forbid."

"All right, so he's good-looking," Zora said, handing back the *Forbes* magazine, and then surrendering herself to the wonderful massage Alejandro was performing on her back and shoulders. This was day two of Melanie's relentless campaign.

"Don't forget *rich*," Melanie reminded her as she too let her eyes drift while a hunky masseur worked knots out of places she had long forgotten existed.

"C'mon, Mel. You oughta know by now that I'm not impressed by a man's bank account. The brotha

I want in my life has to have a good heart and won't feel threatened by a strong woman with her own bling. I'm so over men who try to make me feel bad for being independent."

Melanie laughed. "Oh, I musta hit the sistagirl nerve. I feel ya."

Zora chuckled. "Nah, girl. I'm just keepin' it real. I get more grief from men about the money I'm pullin' down than a little bit. The few relationships I have been in all start the same. 'Baby, you know I looove you,'" she imitated with fake, deep baritone. "'I don't care about you making that long money. Just long as you're bringing all that sweet lovin' to me.'"

Melanie cracked up.

"Don't act like I'm the only one. You're not exactly broke, either."

One side of Melanie's lips quirked up. "I realize as successful women, we have a unique set of hurdles to deal with. But we *can* get over them."

Zora peeled open one eye to stare at the friend lying on the massage table next to her. In the brief silence that followed, she thought how hypocritical Melanie was.

"I'm telling you, Zora. You and Jaxon Landon will hit it off," Melanie insisted, hammering the wild idea that Zora was the perfect woman to really reel in Jaxon Landon. Of course she was going on nothing more than a hunch, but her hunches had a

95 percent batting average. There was also a lot of luck riding on this, too. Zora was perhaps one of the few women in elite New York circles who hadn't gotten wind of Jaxon's reputation.

And what a reputation it was.

The women who had been with Jaxon had described him as a certified sex freak and bragged that he had a libido to put the Energizer bunny to shame. He wasn't opposed to doing it anytime and anyplace. Normally, Melanie wouldn't take on a client with such a voracious sexual appetite. They were usually too hard, if not impossible, to tame.

But to Zora, there was just something about Melanie's instincts that told her she was on the right track. The two women had met back in Melanie's brief stint modeling. She had liked Zora instantly. She wasn't like the other girls in the house where they lived with other models. She had a real brain in her head and it didn't surprise her in the least at just how fast the world and the fashion industry fell in love with her. It also didn't surprise her that Zora turned the platform into an enormous business opportunity.

"Just meet him," Melanie said, sounding sooo close to begging. "What harm is there in just meeting the man?"

Zora released a long sigh. Her resistance was starting to wear down.

"It can be at a party. You come separately and leave separately. We can make it as casual as you want."

Another sigh.

"Trust me." Melanie made one last desperate plea. "You'll thank me for it at your wedding."

Zora laughed at the unlikely notion.

"There's just one thing."

"Aha! I knew there was a catch. What is it? He has a tribe of children by half a dozen women?"

"It's nothing like that." Melanie frowned and then pulled herself up into a sitting position while clutching her towel.

Zora picked up her friend's hesitation and felt the hair on the back of her neck stand up. "All right. Then what?"

Melanie shrugged as if to suggest that it really wasn't such a big deal. "I just need for you *not* to tell him…you know."

Zora signaled for Alejandro to stop rubbing her shoulders. "No. I don't know. Why don't you just spit it out?"

"Let's just say that Jaxon doesn't know that I'm setting this…meeting up."

Zora closed her eyes to prevent herself from rolling them out the back of her head. "A blind date? You're trying to set up a blind date?"

Melanie's smile returned and grew even wider. "Remember. You'll thank me on your wedding day."

Zora's eyes rolled again. "Something tells me that I highly doubt that."

Chapter 3

Jaxon was *not* looking forward to his grandparents' sixtieth wedding anniversary.

It didn't help that he'd almost forgotten about it. It was his crack secretary, Janine, who had cleared his schedule, bought a gift and reminded him that he would probably need to rehire his fake fiancée for a repeat performance or come up with a plausible lie to why Kitty was a no-show.

It was an irritating inconvenience, but one that he would grin and bear for at least a couple of hours.

When he placed a call backstage to the Velvet Rope, Kitty reacted to his invitation like she had just won the lottery. In a way maybe she did. He'd promised her a cool $5K for the night. No, he didn't need to pay for a date, but knowing Kitty's financial situation with her grandma made him feel like he wasn't such a hard-ass like many believed. Plus, he would get another kick out of seeing Carlton sputter and stew in his own indignation.

It would probably be the highlight of his night.

He left his Manhattan high-rise a little past six o'clock, already anxious for the night to speed by. In his apartment lobby, Alfred tipped his hat and wished him a good evening. Jaxon highly doubted that was even possible.

Kwan, his new twenty-one-year-old driver, greeted him at the curb with his Maybach 62. He wore a penguin suit that looked as though it was three sizes too big and a hat that looked even bigger than that. Each time Jaxon saw the kid, he questioned his decision to hire him, but there was just something about the young man's exuberance for the job that won him over.

Of course, the brother also tried his patience with his incredible knack for getting lost in a city he claimed to have lived in his entire life. That took a certain talent. And Jaxon could just forget about Kwan reading or understanding the GPS system in the car. Words like south, east, west or north were all met with the same blank stare. And if Jaxon combined them, southeast, northwest, Kwan looked ready to cry. So it was just best to keep it simple with oldies but goodies like make a left or a right that garnered the best results.

An hour later they made it to Brooklyn with only two wrong turns to which Jaxon had to listen to a ten-minute nonstop apology. Kitty must've been waiting by the door, because the bell hadn't stopped jingling when she jerked it open and greeted him with a Texas-size smile.

The only thing that Jaxon wished that Janine had reminded him to do was tell Kitty to dress conservatively. As it was, she wore a cream-colored sequined dress that fortunately or unfortunately turned transparent when the light hit it. Since he was sure that his grandparents still had the habit of paying their electric bill, there just might be a problem with Kitty's attire.

Then again...didn't he hire the curvaceous stripper to be provocative?

"You don't like my dress?" Kitty guessed after a full minute of him dragging his roaming eyes over her body. She prepared for his usual sly criticism only to be blown away by his devastating smile.

"On the contrary. I think you look ravishing." He offered her his arm, and then seemingly produced a single red rose out of thin air. "Shall we go?"

It was on the tip of Kitty's mouth to say that she would follow Jaxon anywhere, but she reined in her childlike fantasy and just accepted his proffered arm with a practiced innocent smile. "After you."

In the car, Jaxon gave Kwan his grandparents' address only to be met with a wide-eyed blank stare.

Jaxon huffed out a weary breath. "Take a right at the corner."

"Right, boss." Kwan started to pull away from the curb only to be blasted by the horn of a passing Bentley.

"We would like to get there in one piece, if you don't mind," Jaxon added.

"Right, boss. I'm on it, boss."

Kwan tried it again.

Another horn blared, but Kwan forced his way into the lane and then flashed his *thanks* by giving them all a two-finger salute.

Jaxon covered his brow with his hand and tried to massage away the tension headache before it started. During the hour-plus drive out to the Hamptons, Kitty and Jaxon shared stiff smiles over a few glasses of champagne. But for the most part Jaxon allowed his mind to wander back in time. Back to when he was nothing more than a skinny thirteen-year-old kid being forced to live with grandparents he hardly knew.

Jaxon's father, Carlton Jr., had himself rebelled against his father's stern, iron hand to forge his own path in the world. His dropping out of Harvard caused a rift between father and son that lasted until the day Jaxon's parents were killed in a tragic home invasion. It was just lucky that Jaxon had been spending the night at a friend's house the evening of his parents' murder. Otherwise, he would have been home in his own bed, just like his parents had been when two felons broke in the back door and took the most important people in Jaxon's young life.

They say that time heals all wounds—but that was a lie. He missed his parents more today than ever. And the eight years he spent living with his grandparents was like a slow death unto itself. Well, he would be stretching the truth if he included his grandmother. He loved his grandmother. And one of the things he loved most about her was that she knew how and when to stay out of his business.

As far as he was concerned, his grandmother was a class act. He put her beauty and grace high on a pedestal. She was a great confidante, cheerleader and referee between him and Carlton. She never once pressured him into doing anything or becoming anything. Sure, she could get carried away from time to time, feeling faint, needing smelling salts and swearing that her heart could go at any minute. But it was all done with such theatrics that no one really took such declarations seriously.

But Carlton had the ability to get under Jaxon's skin and ride his last nerve effortlessly. Thinking back on it, they had been butting heads from the start, almost as if Jaxon was born to pick up just where his father had left off.

Jaxon was convinced that when Carlton looked at him, he only saw his mother's black skin. Carlton's disapproval of Jaxon's parents' marriage was evident and documented when he didn't bother to attend their wedding in Johannesburg. Carlton was also missing in pictures when Jaxon was born in Los Angeles—or any other special occasion in Jaxon's adolescent years.

Sylvia was there. Always pleading for her son to forgive his father, but never receiving it. Both Carltons were stubborn as mules. It was an unfortunate gene that Jaxon now picked up.

"Are we almost there?" Kitty asked, shifting in her seat. "I have to go to the little girl's room." She set her empty flute down in a holder and then reached for her clutch to retouch her lipstick.

Jaxon performed a cursory glance outside the car window. "We should be there in a few minutes." To be honest, he was a little relieved himself. He never cared for long car rides. They always made him feel as if he was wasting time. Not that he needed to dedicate every minute of the day to making big investment moves, but he needed to be doing *something*. Hell, he wouldn't even mind rustling around in the backseat with Kitty for a few minutes if he could've been sure that Kwan would keep his eyes on the road and not run them into a ditch or up a tree.

Plus, sex always had a way of taking the edge off

whenever he was feeling tense or anxious. He cut a look over at Kitty and knew that she would be down for whatever he was in the mood for, but just then Kwan turned onto Jaxon's grandparents' long, sprawling estate. It was time to suck it up, paste on a smile and ram horns with his grandfather.

There was a short wait, while cars and limos deposited the guests on, of all things, a blue carpet in front of the estate. At first glance, it appeared his grandparents had invited the whole state of New York to what the invitations described as a small get-together. Of course, the Landons never did anything *small*.

Kwan rolled the car to a stop and the valet quickly snatched open the door and offered a hand to assist Kitty. A person would have to have been deaf not to hear the collective shocked gasps when the outdoor lighting hit Kitty's knockout number.

Jaxon stepped out of the car behind Kitty and made a dramatic show of possessively wrapping an arm around the exotic dancer's slim waist. Both he and Kitty thrust up their chins while their eyes and attitude practically dared anyone to say anything about their odd pairing.

"Are you ready for this?" Jaxon queried under his breath.

Kitty leaned closer. "I am if you are."

"Then let's knock them dead." Jaxon slid his free

hand into his pants pocket and escorted Kitty up the royal blue carpet.

"Oops." Kitty sprang out of his grip and stepped back.

Jaxon glanced in time to see a silver tube of lipstick roll down the carpet.

"I forgot to close my clutch."

"I'll get it." Jaxon sprang into action though he felt a little foolish for having to give chase to a tube of lipstick.

Another car pulled up to the curb. The valet immediately opened the door.

Jaxon had stooped to retrieve the shiny lipstick tube when a woman's gorgeous foot encased in a pair of silver stilettos was planted in front of him. Two things seemed to happen. Time stood still and Jaxon had unexpectedly fallen in love...with a foot.

Chapter 4

*O*h. Sweet. Jesus.

It was the only thing that raced across Zora's mind when this black Adonis kneeling before her glanced up—but why was he clutching a tube of... lipstick? *The good ones are all either gay or married.* Still, her brain scrambled trying to remember whether she had ever seen eyes so dark and intense—or even when her heart had pounded so hard. Call her crazy, but she swore an invisible force was tugging at her very soul.

"Good evening, Ms. Campbell," the young valet to her right greeted. Of course it took her a minute to realize that was what was being said since his words entered her head as a jigsaw puzzle. Jaxon Landon's effect on her was just that damn strong.

"Evening good." Zora flushed and then quickly tried to repair the damage. "I mean, good evening."

Jaxon Landon cocked a smile and it seemed as if the whole world stopped.

A stunning, curvaceous woman draped in what can only be best described as a glittering sheer nightgown strolled into the picture. "Oh, sweetie. Thank you. You got it." The woman cut Zora a look that clearly said, "Back the hell off."

Jaxon blinked out of his trance and pulled himself up to his full height. He was so tall that Zora's head tilted back in order to drink him all in. Dressed in an obviously custom-made Armani suit, there was no doubt to even the casual observer that the man was nothing but a wall of hard muscle—not the no-neck, steroids-enhanced kind of muscles, either, but the smooth, toned, rippling kind that a woman would love to have sweating and rocking above *or* beneath her.

"Good evening," Jaxon greeted in a buttery baritone.

She quivered and then realized that she had just had a miniorgasm in front of at least a thousand people. Her face warmed another ten degrees. Zora, like the woman behind him, stood just below the man's mountainous shoulders. Staring at the width of his chest was making her light-headed. Or was that from the lack of food? It certainly couldn't be due to lack of oxygen. They were standing outside.

Two truths suddenly crystallized in Zora's mind. One: she was very much a woman. Two: she was horny as hell.

She flashed the handsome giant a wobbly smile. Jaxon made her feel like a lamb, meekly standing before the king of the jungle. One move and she was doomed—hopefully in a good way. As if he'd heard her private thoughts, the Lion King flashed the sexiest smile she had ever seen on a man.

"We better go in," the glittering woman said. Irritation made her feline voice pitchy. "We're holding up the line."

Hold up. What the hell? Zora was two seconds from scalping this glittering heiffa when she remembered not only *who* she was, but *where* she was. Still, just how was it that the man that was supposed to be *her* date tonight was there with another woman?

Jaxon extended an arm to his date and waltzed off.

Zora glanced around, her face burning with embarrassment. Now *she* was holding up the line. As much as she wanted to, she couldn't just turn back around and hightail it out of there. Her car had already been driven off. One thing she could do was *murder* a certain matchmaker with her bare hands.

Having no choice but to walk behind Jaxon and *his date,* Zora watched Jaxon's smooth, sexy stroll attract many coveted gazes like a magnet. Confirmation that Zora wasn't the only one caught up in his spell.

In a weird way, she didn't mind the rear view because it was just as good as the front. Zora's gaze shifted to the woman glued to his side and it was almost as if she could feel her expensive manicured nails turn into cat claws. *The good ones are always taken—this one* by a woman who looked as if she charged by the hour. Even though she was surprised by her own cattiness, Zora couldn't stop herself from going there. Just as she couldn't stop her gaze from tracking the mysterious giant once they all made it into the Landons' palatial mansion.

Everything about the place screamed money and prestige. It was easily as luxurious as the famous Biltmore Estate. As was the norm for the Hamptons, the home was meant to impress and it more than exceeded. There were wall-to-wall people milling about, talking, laughing and dancing. It definitely wasn't the type of party one would arrange to meet for a blind date—even one who brings a date on a date.

Wait until I get my hands on Melanie. Still, she should've known better. This kind of crazy stuff happened all the time in the dating world. People don't just meet handsome, intelligent, charismatic millionaires all willy-nilly like Melanie made it seem. The truth of the matter was that whole speech about Zora needing more than a career to keep her warm at night, and even that absurd notion of her thanking Melanie on her wedding day for this hook up, had actually penetrated and, well, it'd gotten her hopes up. Instead, this evening looked as though it was just going to be a waste of time.

She hated wasting time. Not that she needed to be dedicating every minute of the day to making money, but she needed to be doing *something*.

Parties weren't normally her thing. Most of the time people just smooched and bragged about their fortunate status in life—each one feeling like they needed to top the other. Nothing was too silly or over-the-top. Nothing was too brash or shameless. Such things bored the living hell out of her. Zora spent two hours washing, waxing and buffing for tonight when she could've just curled up on the couch with a half pint of sorbet and watched *Project Runway*.

Ten minutes in, Zora was ready to call it a night, but she told herself that she was going to stay until she found Melanie. She'd promised to be here, but then again she had also promised her a date. Hedge-fund gurus and technology geniuses weren't her usual crowd. That wasn't to say that people didn't know her. Plenty of men *and* women stopped her to tell her how much they loved her work or gushed over how she was even more beautiful in person.

She dismissed such talk as polite conversation. It was simply what people said to models. In truth, she was no more or less beautiful than most of the women here. Women who went through great expense to obliterate anything that was even thinking about turning into a wrinkle and waged a full-scale war against cellulite, by vacuuming out every extra ounce of fat they could find.

Sure, it was hard to tell when some of them were smiling from time to time, but apparently a movable face was considered sooo overrated. When anyone asked how she knew the Landons, Zora would fake seeing a companion and excuse herself from the conversation. What else could she do? She couldn't very well tell them that she didn't know them or explain why she was crashing their sixtieth anniversary party. She did have *some* pride.

Thirty minutes in, Zora glanced at her jeweled watch. *Ten more minutes,* she promised herself. She'd do one more circle through the crowd and if she didn't see Melanie then that would be just too damn bad. She had fulfilled her end of this silly bargain.

From across the grand room, Jaxon's black gaze followed Zora Campbell like a laser beam. What was she doing here? How did she know his grandparents? It wasn't that he knew everyone they knew, but…he was intrigued. Mainly because back in day he had what he would suppose was a little crush on the supermodel. Hell, ten years ago, Zora Campbell's image was everywhere: on sports magazines, on sexy lingerie covers and a few provocative perfume ads. He remembered one particular provocative Victoria's Secret pose on a Times Square billboard that left little to the imagination that made him and every red-blooded male give her a *hard* salute whenever they walked by.

He couldn't believe that all these years later, she still had the same effect on him. Hell, he could barely get two words out of his mouth outside. No doubt, he came off like just another one of her love-struck fans.

When it came to women, Jaxon had always played his cards close to the chest. He never wanted to show his hand early, if at all. Now here he was, a grown man and certainly an expert at reading and charming women, stumped at what his play should be when he managed to make his way back over to her—hopefully without Kitty attached to his hip. Surely Kitty would understand; after all, she was being paid for her service tonight. It was just the fact that nobody else knew of their charade and it would be more than a bit awkward to flirt in front of a crowd that thought he was engaged.

Talk about a tangled web.

Still, there was no way in the world he was going to pass up this opportunity to talk to *the* Zora Campbell.

"Sweetheart? Sweetheart, did you hear me?" Kitty hip-bumped Jaxon back into reality and flashed him a concerned smile.

Jaxon controlled his irritation and lowered his gaze to Kitty.

"They're asking whether we're thinking about a fall or winter wedding."

Hell, he hadn't even noticed the friends and colleagues that had gathered in a half circle around them. "It's whatever you want, baby." He flashed them a rare smile and then brushed a kiss against Kitty's right temple. Why not? She was just doing what he'd paid her to do: keep up the pretense in order to drive Carlton crazy.

But tonight, his plan may have been ill-timed.

"Jaxon, you slick dog." Richard descended out of nowhere and whacked Jaxon on the back. "I had no idea that you'd decided to make an honest woman out of Ms. Kitty." He tilted his glass of brandy before adding, "I don't know about anyone else but I'm certainly going to miss your act down at the Velvet Rope."

Debra Stinson, Sylvia's oldest and best friend, inquired with a silver knitted brow. "The Velvet Rope?"

The other men in the group glanced around as if they were suddenly fascinated with the mansion's high ceilings.

Everyone except Richard. "It's a gentleman's

club," he answered, smiling. "And the best one in Manhattan I might add."

Mrs. Stinson gasped as her eyes widened. "You mean…" She swung her head back toward Jaxon.

Still cool, Jaxon returned her smile. "What can I say? I'm a man who sees what he likes and goes after it. No matter where it is." He glanced across the room.

"Well, I, it's… Oh, dear." Ms. Stinson's hand fanned herself while her face darkened.

If Richard's goal was to embarrass Kitty or Jaxon, he was sorely disappointed as the newly engaged couple wrapped their arms around each other and shared another tender kiss. "It doesn't bother me what Kitty does for a living. As long as she brings all those fun little costumes home."

Mrs. Stinson's voice spiked. "You mean that she still, um, dances?"

Kitty's smile ballooned. "Of course I do." She glanced up at Jaxon. "And my baby here is still my best tipper."

Mrs. Stinson looked scandalized, blinking and spluttering. "D-does your grandfather know about this?"

"Carlton?" Jaxon's lips quirked up. "He's thrilled about the whole thing." He lied, but again his gaze flew over Kitty's head and toward Zora Campbell. To his surprise, her eyes locked on him, as well.

To his right, Richard followed Jaxon's stare.

"My, my, my," Richard said awestruck. "Is that who I think it is?"

A few more heads whipped in the ex-supermodel's direction.

"Zora Campbell." Richard's whiskey voice hugged the name a little too much to Jaxon's liking. He then cocked his head at Jaxon as if he was recalling a memory. Most likely an old frat party memory where Jaxon had drunkenly admitted that he thought Zora Campbell was hands-down sexier than Tyra Banks or Halle Berry any day of the week. Finally a small smile curled Richard's lips. "Excuse me," he said. "But I think Ms. Campbell looks as though she could use some company."

Jaxon clenched his jaw, but could do nothing but watch this smooth snake slither across the room.

"She's here," Melanie whispered into Sylvia Landon's ear after sprinting across the room in a pair of red Manolo Blahniks.

"Where?" Sylvia's head whipped around the room, her eyes wide as she scanned the perimeter. In no time flat her gaze zeroed in on the supermodel on the opposite side of the grand room. "Oh. She's even more stunning in person," she complimented. "Jaxon should love her." Sylvia glanced over at Melanie. "Do we know whether he's seen her yet?"

"I don't—"

"Oh, he's seen her all right." Veronica dipped

into the conversation, having popped up out of nowhere. "Everyone's gossiping about how his tongue damn near rolled out of his head outside."

Melanie and Sylvia turned toward Veronica. Sylvia with hope and Melanie with dread. If Zora had already run into Jaxon, there was a good chance that she'd also run into his *date*.

Sylvia fluttered a hand over her heart. "Good. We may actually pull this off." She looked as if she would swoon with relief.

Veronica confirmed Melanie's fears. "It's also circulating that his fiancée wasn't looking too pleased, I might add."

"That's also good news," Sylvia said with a roll of her eyes.

Carlton noticed his wife's distraction. "What are you *young* ladies talking about?" His eyes twinkled as he slid an arm around his wife's slim waist.

"Oh, nothing, dear." Sylvia kissed his cheek and hoped that he wouldn't pry any deeper into their conversation. It was a rare night for him to be in a good mood. The last thing she wanted to do was spoil it. Nothing could do that faster than a discussion about their rebellious grandson.

Carlton's eyes narrowed but a playful smile tugged his lips. After sixty years of marriage, he knew when his wife was lying. Given the occasion, his twinkling eyes let her know that he was going to let her get away with whatever scheme she was cooking up—for now. "How about I just refresh your drink, dear?" he asked.

"That's an excellent idea." The look and smile they shared radiated a deep love that had sustained them for more than a half century. A lot of the guests caught the intimate moment, elbowed one another and shared knowing smiles.

At eighty-two, Sylvia was still the envy of most of her friends—mainly because all of them had suffered through at least one divorce. Love in the rich lane was usually short-term. As far as their friends were concerned, Sylvia and Carlton had somehow pulled off a miracle.

Once Carlton left to refresh her drink and was out of earshot, Sylvia quickly turned toward Melanie. "Okay. So what do we do?"

"Well, first thing we need to do is unhook Jaxon's current fiancée from his arm so I can properly introduce him to Zora," Melanie said. Of course her brain was still scrambling for an explanation for Jaxon's fiancée. She had hoped to clear up all the hiccups for this hook up, but that no longer looked like that was viable option.

Sylvia winked. "I know just the thing. I'll signal you when the coast is clear."

Before Melanie could question her further, Sylvia gathered one side of her silver gown and made a beeline toward Jaxon and Kitty. Melanie noted that for an eighty-two-year-old, the woman still moved pretty quickly.

Carlton returned, carrying two flutes of champagne. He glanced at Melanie and then looked around as if double-checking to see if this was the spot he'd left his wife. "Now where did she run off to?"

Melanie just smiled and shrugged her shoulders. The best thing to do in her position was to play dumb. "Won't you excuse me for a moment, Mr. Landon?" Instead of waiting for an answer, she hightailed it the opposite direction.

"Jaxon, baby. You made it," Sylvia said, easing her way in between him and his date.

Jaxon jerked his gaze from the back of Richard's head. His usually stoic face softened with a genuine smile. "I wouldn't have missed it for the world." He leaned forward and pressed a kiss against his grandmother's upturned cheek. "Happy anniversary, Grans." He reached inside his jacket pocket and removed a thin ivory box with a glittering blue bow.

"Oh, bless Janine's heart," she said, taking the gift. "I'm sure that she was able to get us something wonderful. She has exceptional taste."

Jaxon chuckled. There was no use in pretending that he had anything to do with picking out the gift. His grandmother would see straight through such a lie. "You know I love you, Grandma."

"Of course I do, sweetie." She leaned into his

side to revel in the warmth of his love. She took great pleasure in being one of the few people Jaxon showered with genuine affection. On Wall Street he showcased his cutthroat, take-no-prisoners side. As far as friends were concerned, Jaxon believed the fewer of those the better. Of course, he had the opposite view when it came to women.

Reluctantly, Sylvia turned her attention to Kitty, but she made sure that she kept her smile at all the appropriate angles. "Kitty, *darling.* Now that you're going to be a part of the family soon, what do you say that I give you an official tour of the house?"

Kitty blinked. "What? Now?" She glanced around the crowded room. "I wouldn't want to take you from all of your guests."

Sylvia waved off the comment. "Don't be silly. It shouldn't take us long." *Only about an hour.* "Plus, I can introduce you to some important people—make sure you meet all the right people. It's important *if* you're going to become a Landon."

"Well, I, uh…" Kitty glanced up toward Jaxon for guidance.

He only shrugged. "You might as well go. Grans never takes no for an answer."

Kitty's mouth dipped with disappointment.

"Don't act like I'm the only one," Sylvia said, waving a finger.

Jaxon laughed. His devastating smile drew female gazes like moths to a flame.

"C'mon, dear." Sylvia took Kitty's arm and looped it through her own. "I can't wait to show you some of the precious artwork we have in the east wing." She led the young beauty off while surreptitiously finding Melanie Harte in the crowd and giving her a "Coast is clear" head nod.

Melanie smiled at the sly fox and then turned to look for her own target.

Chapter 5

"Ms. Campbell, right?"

Zora turned away from a chatty *New York Times* writer and toward an immaculate devil, dressed in black and looking as dangerous as the serpent in the Garden in Eden. One thing was for certain, he was handsome. No doubt about it. "I'm afraid that you have me at a disadvantage. You are…?"

"In love," he countered, reaching for her hand and then lifting it to brush a light kiss against her knuckles.

Zora smiled and said, "Smooth. I'll give you that."

"It's the truth," he insisted. "I've been a fan of your work for quite some time."

"Thank you." She removed her hand from his soft grip and was ready to move on.

"Aah." He bobbed his head. "Strike one."

"Excuse me?" she said, still managing to hold on to a polite smile.

"I'd say that judging by your reaction that you've probably heard that 'fan of your work' line at least a thousand times."

She chuckled. "Actually—more like a million."

"Awww, man. I knew it." He rolled his eyes and shook his head. "Well, we can just rewind the clock and start all over."

"We can?"

He shrugged. "It's a little trick I learned back in college. Watch." He turned, straightened his shoulders and then made a slow spin back around on his heels. This time when he faced her, his smile was blinding and his eyes twinkled. "Hello, there. I, uh, saw you from across the room and I just had to come over and introduce myself," he said in his best debonair voice.

"Oh, is that right?" Zora chuckled.

"Absolutely." He stepped closer. "You're easily *the* most beautiful woman in the room. Mind if I ask your name?"

Laughing, Zora started to answer, but was stalled when he placed a silencing finger against her red lips.

"Don't tell me. Let me guess." He pressed. "Your face. Your eyes. That smile. Surely your name couldn't be anything other than *Beautiful*. No, no, no. *Bella*. Italian for beautiful." He winked. "If I'm wrong, don't tell me because you will always be *Bella* to me."

Zora had to admit that she was charmed by this handsome devil. At least *he* didn't appear to have a date with him. "I'm flattered," she said, allowing him to reclaim her hand for another brush of his lips. "And now that we know who *I* am…?"

"Richard," he supplied. "Richard Myers. If you're with this crowd, I'm sure you may have heard of me."

Zora winced as her smile turned sheepish.

"Annnd…maybe not," he corrected with an awkward laugh. "Wow. I guess I just sounded like a pompous ass."

"Sorry," Zora said. "I, uh, actually don't know that many people here."

"Oh?" He turned as another waiter waltzed by and deftly retrieved two champagne flutes. "Are you here with someone?"

"No. Not really."

Richard spiked one brow.

"I was supposed to meet someone here." Her gaze jumped over his shoulder.

Richard followed her gaze and found himself in Jaxon's line of fire. If looks could kill this whole house would have been taped off as a homicide scene. Richard's smile bloomed even wider as he shifted his attention back toward Zora, but she was already pretending to be interested in the little tune twinkling from the piano player. "Sooo. You're a friend of Jaxon's?" he asked.

"Hmm? Oh, no." She flashed her million-dollar smile. "In fact, I only just met him a few minutes ago outside. Sort of. I don't know if you could really classify that as *meeting* him—more like an awkward hello." Zora was vaguely aware that she was rambling.

Richard nodded. His gaze lingered as if to weigh whether she was telling the truth. "Well, I suppose that this is the perfect venue to show off his new *fiancée*."

"His...fiancée?" she asked, making sure that she hadn't misunderstood.

From her reaction, Richard concluded the model had lied when she said that she didn't know Jaxon.

"Yes," he insisted. His mind was already whirling with different scenarios on how to pluck this beautiful rose right from beneath Jaxon's nose. "I see you're just as shocked as the rest of us. I, for one, never thought of Jaxon as the settling down type. You know his motto. 'So many women, so little time.'" Richard chuckled, despite the fact that he was the only one laughing.

Shocked wasn't the word that described what Zora was feeling—*pissed* seemed more fitting. Just then Melanie tapped Zora's shoulder. Zora whipped her head around and leveled Melanie with a murderous look.

Melanie's eyes widened as she took a step back. "Is there a problem?"

"You're damn right there's a problem," Zora hissed but then pivoted back toward Richard with a sweet-as-honey smile. "Could you please excuse us for a moment?" she asked Richard.

"No. No. Not at all." He stepped back and then suggested, "I'll see about wrangling up some hors d'oeuvres."

"Sounds great." Zora smiled, but then dropped it when she snatched Melanie's hand and led her a few feet away. "What in the *hell* is going on? Is this some kind of sick joke?"

"Okay. I know that you might be a little angry right now," Melanie said gently, hoping to smooth over this unfortunate hiccup.

"Engaged?" Zora hissed, ignoring Melanie placating tone. "Are you kidding me? The man is *engaged?*"

Melanie's eyes widened like a little girl caught with her hand in the cookie jar. "Okay. I know that might seem like a little snag—"

"A *snag?*" Zora reached over and literally knocked on the woman's head. "Hello? Is anybody in there? A *snag* would be if the man was running late for our *date* or that he talked with a lisp. A fiancée is more than a *snag,* it's a major problem."

"All right. Just calm down."

"I can't calm down." Zora jerked back. "What?

You were trying to keep it a secret? Oh, God, did this man hire you because he's—he's what?—looking for some chick on the side?" Then she was hit with another possibility. "Are they swingers?" she gasped. "Was I supposed to be both of their dates?"

"What? No." Melanie waved her hands as if that would help erase the notion from Zora's head. "It's nothing like that at all. It's—"

"You know what? I don't care." Zora shook her head and started to move away. "I knew I shouldn't have agreed to this. Next time, I'll follow my instincts."

"Wait, Zora. Let me explain." Melanie reached for her hand, but Zora jerked it out of her reach and kept it moving.

"Damn it!" Melanie stomped her foot. Her plans were blowing up in her face even before she could put them to work.

Now untangled from his *fiancée,* Jaxon watched Zora Campbell and Melanie Harte with a growing interest. Well, more like he was watching Zora with interest. Clearly she was upset about something because it caused these two little cute lines to bunch over the ridge of her nose.

Next thing he knew, she was on the move—and fast. Her long legs carried her to the front door in a blink of an eye. He covered the same distance in a close second. "Leaving so soon?"

Zora stopped cold, causing Jaxon to slam against her back. The impact propelled her into motion again, but a quick-thinking Jaxon extended an arm and caught her around the waist. She gasped at what felt like a steel band latching around her waist. When she was pulled back against a solid wall of muscles, she lost the ability to get her legs or her mind to work properly.

"Easy now."

Zora closed her eyes at the way his buttery baritone drifted over the shell of her ear. Another delicious quiver shimmied up her center. What kind of man could make a woman come just by the sound of his voice?

A dangerous man.

The answer should have been enough to get Zora to hightail it out of there. Yet again, there was some faulty wiring between her head and her legs because she remained rooted where she stood. Of course it might have something to do with the fact that his arm was still locked around her waist—not to mention she could feel her own effect on him rising up against the curve of her butt. Needless to say she was impressed.

Very impressed.

"Are you all right?" he asked, amused.

Zora's body temperature spiked a good ten degrees. He *knew* that she could feel his hard-on against her ass and he was clearly waiting to see what her next move would be. She knew what it *should* be, but damn, the last thing she felt like doing was the *right* thing.

Finally, she drew a deep breath and pushed at his arm for him to release her.

He complied, allowing his arm to swing down to his side. When she turned around, like he knew she would, he was propped comfortably against a white marble pillar and staring at her like a predator playing with his food.

"Jaxon Landon," he introduced.

"Zora Campbell."

"Nice to *officially* meet you," he said. His gaze took its time climbing her every curve. When it finally rested on her face, a soft smile eased the corners of his lips and unbelievably his eyes grew darker. "Had I known that we had such a beautiful friend of the family, I might've come home more often."

She smiled, mainly because it was the only thing she could manage to do and even that had her worrying whether she was beginning to look like a plastic idiot.

"You're not leaving, are you? You just got here."

"I, um." She coughed and cleared her throat. "Let's just say there's been a change of plans." Even though she wanted to appear as cool and aloof as he was right now, she couldn't stop herself from drinking him in—every magnificent, glorious inch of him.

Lawd, have mercy.

Jaxon hiked a single groomed brow. "I hate to hear that. More importantly, I hate to see you leave before we had the chance to get know each other…*better.*"

Their eyes locked.

This was the part where reason and logic should've been injected, but Zora was having problems in those departments, as well. To hell with his fiancée, she wasn't around now.

"How come you're not draped across some lucky bastard's arm tonight?" he asked.

She smiled, wondering how he would've taken it if he'd known that he was supposed to be that lucky bastard. "Not all women need to be *draped* on a man's arm," she stated.

"True," he conceded. "But all jewels should." His dark gaze continued to drink her in. The crowd around them continued to thicken. Zora moved closer toward Jaxon and then suffered the consequences of her body tingling and pulsing like crazy. Zora had never experienced anything like it before. Everything about the man oozed sex: his scent, his eyes, his shoulders, his chest.

Then he did something that she would have never expected. He reached out and removed the bejeweled hair clip from the back of her head. Her thick, black hair fell down around her shoulders like a curtain.

"There. That's better." His smile mesmerized her. "You should always wear your hair down. It makes you…irresistible." His hand caressed her face and before she knew it, the pad of his thumb drifted beneath the lining of her bottom lip. No doubt about it, her panties were dampening by the second.

Zora watched his sexy lips like a dieter standing before a three-tier chocolate cake. If she wasn't mistaken, she might have even licked her lips.

"I have to tell you, Ms. Campbell—"

"Zora."

"I have to tell you—*Zora*—that I have half a mind to toss you over my shoulder and carry you out of here." His smile grew even sexier. "And if you keep looking at me like that, that's exactly what's going to happen."

Snap out of it, Zora's brain screamed, but her body ignored her. She was acting like a…she didn't know what…with an engaged man.

Engaged isn't married, the small voice in the back of her head reminded her.

She swallowed hard at that very real fact, but was she really the type of girl to make a play for another woman's man?

Jaxon looked around, frowned at the growing crowd. "What do you say that we go somewhere where it's a little more private?" His hand left her face only to pop back up on her bare shoulder. She would have expected such a large hand to be heavy, but it was as light as a feather and yet powerful enough to stroke a lustful fire to life.

"It's a big house," he continued, his voice now a low, husky whisper. "Big enough for two people to get lost."

Zora sank deeper into this man's trance, a willing lamb trotting docilely to the slaughterhouse.

"I do have to warn you," he said, reaching for her hand and then bringing it up to his lips. "I have quite a reputation."

"Is that right?" she asked silkily.

He nodded. "Unfortunately, *most* of it is true."

His confession only turned her on more. Then again, bad boys always had a way of turning a good girl's head. "In that case, I heard a rumor tonight," she said, surprised by her own courage to broach the subject. "It involved you and the woman you escorted here."

He sighed, but his smile remained. "I was afraid of that."

"I believe it was something along the lines of her being your, um…now, what's that word I'm thinking of?" She made a show of rolling her eyes toward the ceiling as if in deep thought. "Oh, yeah." Zora snapped her fingers. "Fiancée."

Unfazed, but amused, Jaxon said, "It's complicated—but I'll be more than happy to explain it to you if you agree to meet me in west-wing upstairs library. Second door on the right from the spiral staircase. How about—in one hour?"

Zora hesitated.

Jaxon leaned down, whispered, "Say yes."

His hand fell from her shoulder and brushed against the small of her back. She shuttered with another miniorgasm. What the hell would happen to her if she allowed him to really touch her?

"There you are!" Richard's voice blasted like a sonic boom.

Zora leaped away from Jaxon as Richard swooped in, cheesing like a Cheshire cat but shooting silver bullets dead at Jaxon.

"Should've known you would be around the most beautiful woman in the room. I guess old habits are hard to break, huh, Jaxon? I mean with you now being off the market and all."

Jaxon's hard glare turned to black ice.

Richard held out a small plate toward Zora. "Hors d'oeuvres?"

Zora cleared her throat and reached for a cube of fancy cheese, but kept her eyes diverted. She really needed a moment to collect herself or fan herself off. Better yet, maybe she needed a cold shower.

"By the way," Richard said, taking a stand next to Zora as if staking a claim, "where is the future Mrs. Landon anyway? Surely she knows better than to let you roam without a leash."

Jaxon's eyes shifted back to Zora just as she looked up. "Don't worry, my future wife is closer than you think." The statement took all three of them by surprise. But the ever cool Jaxon was the first to recover. "If you two will excuse me."

"Absolutely," Richard said flatly.

Jaxon held up a slender finger, reminding Zora of the one-hour request and then he turned and maneuvered back into the herding crowd.

Zora watched him go with an unexplainable longing for his quick return. Her emotions must've been written on her face because when she glanced over at Richard, he was shaking his head. "What?"

"Charming devil, isn't he?"

There was no point in trying to pretend she didn't know who he was talking about. "He is."

Richard looked pleased by her honesty. "Then just remember that it's never a fair game when you play with the devil."

Zora's gaze cut back across the room just when Jaxon's fiancée returned to his side. After delivering a quick kiss to the glittering woman's cheek, he glanced up. His black, intense gaze zeroed on Zora like a laser beam. "One hour," he mouthed.

The temperature in the room easily hiked another ten degrees—at least to the point where Zora hand-fanned herself in order to cool off.

Across the room, Melanie, Veronica, Jessica and Vincent all captured the public—yet intimate—moment between Zora and Jaxon and then shared knowing smiles.

"Looks like you're going to get your miracle after all," Vincent deadpanned.

Melanie beamed. "Let the church say 'amen.'"

"Amen," Veronica and Jessica chimed as they clinked their champagne glasses together, and then continued to watch the evening soap opera unfold.

Chapter 6

I'm not meeting him in that library.

Zora lost count how many times she told herself that. She also reasoned that she had stayed at the party long enough and that she should call it a night. Yet, she never made another move toward the front door—and no matter where she was at the party, she was *very* aware of her proximity to Jaxon Landon. She couldn't help it. The man was like a six-foot-four magnet.

Still, to her right, handsome Richard Myers was working overtime trying to pull off what Jaxon had done in mere seconds. Maybe if it had been any other night, she would have given him some play—

but with Jaxon Landon in the room, Richard could never be more than second best.

Within the past hour, the crowd changed the words to the traditional "Happy Birthday" song to sing "Happy Anniversary." At the song's conclusion, Tony Bennett magically appeared next to the pianist and crooned "The Best Is Yet to Come." There wasn't a dry eye in the place when Carlton Landon took his wife into his arms and glided across the grand room floor while singing along in Sylvia's ear.

The moment made for a perfect modern fairy tale. Zora thought about her parents and how their love also seemed to grow with each passing day. Envy plus a touch of jealousy pricked her heart. Such lifelong soul mates were now few and far between. Of course one would have to put themselves out there if they ever hoped to find their happily-ever-after.

Zora's gaze floated over to Melanie Harte—who held up a flute of champagne in a silent toast. No doubt her best bud knew *exactly* why she was still at the party. The missing puzzle piece was why would she fix her up with someone who was already engaged? Her pride prevented her from asking right now, especially since she'd cursed her out an hour ago.

Why am I still here?

Every time the question drifted through Zora's head she couldn't come up with a good answer. Her night was a bust, her date showed up with a fiancée, and she hardly knew anyone at this party.

Yet—there she was. Laughing and cheesing on Richard Myers's arm like she was having the time of her life. Okay. Maybe a small part of her wanted to put on a show for Jaxon Landon—to try and make him as interested in her as she was in him. Though, she still didn't know why.

"You know this is the perfect time for us to make a move," Richard whispered.

Zora frowned, not sure that she understood his meaning. She glanced back over her shoulder and up into his smiling face.

"I'd love nothing better than to get a little one-on-one time with you," he said. His meaning twinkled in his eyes.

Despite her heavy flirting, Zora wasn't half as charmed by Richard as he thought she was, and the last thing she wanted to do was lead him on any further than she probably already had.

But then she sensed it.

Jaxon's heavy and intense gaze felt like a physical thing even from across the room. Like she had most of the evening, she reveled in any attention he tossed her way. Before she knew it, she was smiling at Richard and agreeing to him leading her through the thick crowd.

Across the room, Veronica leaned toward her aunt. "Where is she going?"

Melanie shook her head while trying not to panic. But then she took one look at Jaxon and saw raw jealousy flicker across his face. "Don't worry. Clearly, my girl knows exactly what's she doing."

Veronica shook her head. "If you say so."

Zora had no idea where Richard was taking her, but she vowed that if it was too far that she would fake having to run to the bathroom and do a complete 180. Turned out, he led her down a hall to a billiard room just a couple doors down. "If you hoped to challenge me to a game of pool, I have to warn you that I'm not much of a player," she joked.

Richard laughed. "Trust me," he said, looking steadily into her eyes. "The last thing I'm interested in is playing *games* with you."

His seriousness melted the playful smile right off Zora's face. "Richard…I may have given you the wrong impression. I—"

With a sly smile, Richard pressed a finger against Zora's cherry-red lips. "The only impression I have is that of a beautiful, intelligent woman that has been gracious enough to spend a little time with me." He broke out in a wide smile. "I have to tell you that I thought tonight was going to be a big snoozer. I mean, I like the Landons well enough. Our families have been more or less friends for a good number of years—but I anticipated a dull evening—until I spotted you."

What could she say to that? "Thanks. You're being too kind." Zora drew a deep breath and then tried again. "But the truth is—"

"I'm not sure that I'm interested in the truth," he said bluntly.

Surprised, Zora arched a lone brow.

"I'm no fool," Richard continued with an awkward laugh. "I'm sure a beauty such as yourself has a long line of admirers—including the idiot who stood you up tonight."

She glanced away, cleared her throat.

Richard moved in even closer. "All I'm interested in is the here and now. This one moment in time where I escort you out there onto the terrace—" he indicated the glass doors behind her with a simple nod of his head "—and we'll look up at the stars and listen to the music drifting from the party. Is that too much to ask?"

When he leveled his soft hazel eyes on her, guilt stirred in her heart. The man had been nothing but a perfect gentleman all night while she, on the other hand, had been actin' like a bitch in heat from the moment she'd laid eyes on Jaxon Landon.

"Well?" he pressed.

"No," she finally said. "It's not too much to ask."

A brighter, wider smile exploded across Richard's handsome face. "Good. Then how about that view?" He offered her his arm and then promptly escorted her out to the terrace.

They had been gone for way too long.

Jaxon's gaze peeled from his dancing grandparents to dart to the hallway where Richard and Zora had disappeared. To say that his imagination ran wild would be putting it mildly. He imagined everything from the two being snuggled up in a dark corner lip-locked to—more. He didn't like any of those scenarios. But each and every one of them was possible with a snake in the grass like Richard Myers.

Kitty leaned up onto her toes and whispered, "What is wrong with you?"

"Um? Nothing." He shoved his near-empty glass of champagne toward her. "Hold this for me. I'll be right back."

"Wait. What?" She grabbed his glass before it dropped and shattered at her feet. When she finally got her bearings and glanced up again, Jaxon was gone. *Now where in the hell is he going?*

Out on the billiard room's balcony, Zora drew in the night's cool air and stared up at the sky. With the soft music in the background and a picture of a clear crescent moon hovering above her, it was the perfect romantic spot—like something out of a movie or an oil painting. Why didn't she take time to enjoy more scenic skylines? Sure she was always on the go, burning both ends of a candle, but surely she could stop every once in a while and drink in the moment.

"Isn't it beautiful?" Richard murmured softly against her ear.

Zora jumped. Somehow she'd forgotten about him. Recovering, she flashed him her million-dollar smile. "It is. Thank you for bringing me out here.

It's…perfect." She sucked in another deep breath and returned her attention to the night's skyline.

Richard eased up behind her. "The only perfect thing I see out here is you."

The man didn't give up. She'd give him that much. "Thanks," she whispered. She tilted up her champagne glass and drained its contents in one long gulp.

Richard's glass stopped halfway to his mouth as he watched her down her drink like a seasoned sailor.

"Aaah. That was good." Zora smacked her lips.

"Would you like another drink?"

"I would love one." She shoved her glass toward him. "Oh, and another one of those cheese-and-sausage thingies," she added. Richard looked a little stunned.

"Yes. Models do eat," she joked.

Richard laughed. "All right. I'll be back," he said, accepting the glass and stepping away.

Zora waved as she watched him walk backward off the terrace and into the billiard room and then finally out of sight. At which point, she rolled her eyes and expelled a long breath. *The things I get myself into.*

Kitty glanced around the crowd and noted that the gorgeous Zora Campbell was missing, as well. She had a sinking feeling in the pit of her stomach. She may be a lot of things, but she was no fool. She saw and felt the kinetic energy charging between Jaxon and the buxom supermodel. Hell, everybody felt it. The question now was what was she going to do about it?

Tony Bennett finished the last few notes to "The Way You Look Tonight" and the glittering crowd applauded. When the next song began, everyone started pairing up to join in the dancing. Being that this wasn't her normal crowd, Kitty wasn't about to just stand in the center of the floor, looking lost and confused. Deciding then and there that she wasn't about to go down without a fight, Kitty maneuvered through the crowd, set the empty champagne flutes on the first tray she came across—then she went in search of her missing *fiancé.*

Jaxon always hated this house. And now that he was faced with trying to guess which room Richard had shut Zora away in, he hated it even more. Searching for the couple would be like trying to find a needle in a haystack. Still, knowing that fact, it didn't stop him from looking.

The first two rooms he checked were dark but after walking around in them, they were mercifully empty. When he pivoted and marched toward the third door, it dawned on him that perhaps he should have some kind of excuse in case he did bust in on Richard and Zora doing God knows what. Some-thing like, "Oh, hey. I thought this room was empty" or, he could play innocent and simply ask, "Hey, what are you two doing in here?" or, his personal favorite, "Dick, get your damn hands off her before I punch your goddamn lights out!"

Yeah. The last one was perfect.

The third door was to his grandfather's favorite billiard room. It was a bit dark, but there was no one…Jaxon's gaze snagged on the open glass door, leading out to the terrace. Curious, he started toward it but was interrupted when Kitty's kittenlike purr floated from behind him.

"There you are!" Her smile lit up her face. "What are you doing in here?" She glanced around. "You're not the only one who could use a break from that crowd, you know." Kitty sashayed over to Jaxon and slid her arms up his massive chest. "In fact, now that I have you all to myself, I can think of a few things we can be doing." She leaned up on her toes and planted a soft, sensuous kiss on his pillow-soft lips.

On the terrace, Zora caught the intimate moment between the engaged couple and felt a sharp kick of jealousy—which was strange, since she had just met the man tonight. Then she realized that if she could see them then it was just a matter of time before one of them saw her.

She quickly stepped to the side behind a potted tree or plant—she didn't know which, but it would do to get herself out of view. But even then she couldn't stop herself from peeking through the leaves for a second look.

It took a minute, but Kitty realized that Jaxon wasn't really responding with the same fever and gusto she was used to. When she broke the kiss and stared into his eyes, she could easily read that his mind was elsewhere. She had a sinking suspicion that she knew where. Well, she certainly knew a few tricks to get a man's attention focused back on her.

"What's the matter, baby? Don't you wanna play?" Her slim fingers made quick work of his shirt.

"Hey, hey." He tried to stop her. "Cut it out. Not here."

"Why not?" Kitty purred, her hands moving from his shirt to his belt. "If memory serves me right, we've done it in stranger places."

Jaxon swiped her hands from his belt only for her to attack his zipper.

"C'mon, sweetie. Don't be a party pooper. It's not like your grandparents are going to walk in on us." She sank to her knees and she reached inside his pants and grabbed hold of his cock.

Jaxon leaped backward. "Kitty, stop."

"Oooh." She climbed back onto her feet. "I love it when you play hard to get."

"Kitty." He waved a finger at her. "Behave."

"No." She playfully tried to bite his finger and

when he jumped, she added an extra push, which caused him to fall back and collapse into a leather upholstered chair. While he looked stunned, Kitty used the moment to her advantage and jumped into his lap and smothered him with kisses.

Wide-eyed, Zora watched the love play with growing envy. She also had the problem of being trapped out on the terrace with the night's cool breeze turning decidedly colder by the second.

"Kitty." Jaxon's warning drifted out onto the terrace, but to Zora's ears it sounded as if his persistent fiancée was wearing down his defenses.

There was some giggling and some moaning while Zora shook her head and rolled her eyes. *Why didn't I go home when I had the chance?* She glanced around and checked out the stone railing. Maybe she could escape by climbing over the damn thing. However when she tiptoed over, she realized that there was no way she was going to manage such a feat in her A-line gown—not without hiking the damn thing up around her waist and possibly flashing her panties and scuffing up her knees.

Zora moved back over to the potted tree and saw Jaxon and his girl playfully wrestling in the chair. *I gotta do something to get out of here.* She looked around again and drew another conclusion: she could crawl out of the open glass door. At least the billiard room was carpeted. No flashing needed and her knees would be protected.

But will I get past them without getting caught?

She didn't have an answer to that, but *a* plan was better than *no* plan. The next thing Zora knew, she was on her hands and knees and crawling as quietly as she could toward the door.

"C'mon, baby, let's play," Kitty whined. "Please?"

"Kitty!"

"Pretty please?"

"Kitty, this is not a good time."

Just keep going. You're almost there.

"It's always a good time, baby." Kitty giggled. "Now, can *big* Jaxon come out and play?"

Zora rolled her eyes but kept crawling. *Melanie is one dead woman.*

"Kitty, you're not listening to me."

"Of course not. You're not saying anything I want to hear, silly."

There was more giggling, but Zora just kept her eye on the prize: the door.

"Ooh. There's big Jaxon." Giggle.

Creep. Creep.

"Kitty—"

"Look how hard he is!"

"Kitty, that's enough!"

Creep. Creep. *Almost there.*

Just then the door burst open and Richard breezed into the room.

"What the—?" Richard's hard gaze swept from Jaxon to Kitty and then softened with relief.

Kitty sprang back, looking guilty as sin and adjusting her gown's shoulder straps.

Jaxon jumped to his feet. However, his pants slid straight down to the floor and his exposed cock stood straight as an arrow. "Shit."

"Damn," Richard said. "I see why you're so popular with the ladies."

"Very funny." Jaxon bent over to grab his pants when his eyes clashed with Zora's on the floor on other side of the pool table.

However, she wasn't exactly looking him in the eye. More like she was stunned at the sheer size of Jaxon's thick, smooth cock. Hell, it looked like a piece of fine art and was hands-down the most beautiful thing she'd seen in a looong time. Slowly, she began to realize that *everyone's* eyes were on her.

"Hi." What else could she say?

Richard cocked his head. "What are you doing down there?"

Zora drew a blank. "Um. That's a good question." She sat back on her knees and then used the billiard table to help herself up off the floor. "I, um." Zora scratched at her brow, trying to search for a plausible excuse, but the only thing she could come up with was to admit the truth. "Well, they seemed to be having a good time—" She gestured toward Jaxon and Kitty without looking at them. "And I didn't want to, um, interrupt…so I was just trying to make my way out…without, um, disturbing them." Her face was red-hot by the time she finished explaining.

Don't look at him. Don't look at him.

Of course, she looked over at Jaxon…and the bastard was actually smiling as he zipped himself back into his pants.

Kitty smirked as she looped an arm around Jaxon's waist. "When you're engaged to a man as fine as Jaxon, it's kinda hard to keep your hands off of him." To emphasize her point, she ran her hand up and down his chest.

Embarrassed, Zora rushed toward the door. "Excuse me."

Richard dropped the two flutes of champagne, trying to stop Zora's exit, but she was way too fast for him. "Zora, wait."

Zora didn't wait. She couldn't. She needed to get the hell out of there.

Chapter 7

Zora did everything she could to forget about her embarrassing night at the Landons' estate, but after two weeks, it was safe to say that nothing worked. It didn't help that every day, since that night, she received two dozen roses. One dozen from Jaxon and a second set from Richard. Both tried to apologize and insisted on taking her out to make up for the embarrassing evening. It reached a point where Zora couldn't stop rolling her eyes every time Monica brought the flowers into her home office. Her place was starting to look like a florist shop or a funeral home—she could not decide which.

Then there was Melanie. She called every hour

on the hour. Zora refused to take any of her calls. In fact, it was probably going to take a long time for their friendship to recover from this.

Though she kept telling herself that she didn't want to know the whole story of why Melanie even thought to set her up with a man that was clearly off the market, another part of her was *dying* to know the 4-1-1—just as there was an itty-bitty part of her that kept replaying the moment when Jaxon Landon's beautiful cock sprang out of his black silk boxers. She couldn't get over how ramrod straight and smooth and polished it looked despite the dim lighting. Hell, sometimes, Zora took creative license and removed all his clothes in her mind and added a bright red cape around his neck.

Ridiculous—yes.

But fitting.

Zora struggled to keep her head out of the clouds, but there were moments where she'd still catch herself fantasizing about what it would have been like to touch it, kiss it, maybe even give it a little ride. She was turning herself on. Of course it was easy to do when one was in a dry spell. Damn, how long had it been?

Zora leaned back in her chair and thought about it. The more months she counted, the deeper her frown became. *Last Thanksgiving?* She shook her head. That couldn't be right. Zora stood up and retrieved her BlackBerry from her purse. For the next several minutes, she flipped through her calendar,

shaking her head. Sure, she was too busy for a com-
mitted relationship, but that didn't mean that she
couldn't have squeezed in at least a couple of booty
calls every now and then.

Sure enough, her calendar confirmed it. Last
Thanksgiving with Calvin Jackson. She gave his
performance one star. Then the horrific experience
crystallized in her mind. His sloppy wet kisses were
like a Saint Bernard mopping her face with its
tongue. Hell, she didn't know what he was trying
to do. Calvin's big NBA hands had pawed and
groped her breasts to the point that she was convinced that they were going to be black and blue by
morning.

And his dick? Forgetaboutit.

Zora had thought he was kidding when he would
jokingly refer to himself as *Millimeter Man.*

He wasn't joking.

The man was small. *Small.* S-M-ALL.

During their wild and crazy two-minute sex-
athon, Calvin really wore the hell out of one corner
of her right thigh. All the while, he kept asking,
"You like that, baby? It feels good, don't it?"

Talk about rather having a V-8.

Zora almost didn't have the heart to tell him that
he wasn't even in.

Keyword—*almost.*

When Calvin was finally so inclined to stick it in,
he came twenty seconds later—with his face a con-

torted hot mess and enough sweat pouring off him that one would've thought he'd just finished playing the final game in the NBA championship. Zora didn't come, not that Calvin cared, but she remembered being relieved that the whole experience was over.

Still, lousy sex was no reason to just throw in the towel. She reached back into her purse and pulled out her pink book. It was time for her to put in an old-fashioned booty call. Maybe that was what had her all screwy and obsessing over Jaxon's cock. She was just horny.

Zora returned to her office desk and started flipping through the pages. Over the years she had collected hundreds if not thousands of men's names and numbers. She certainly hadn't slept with them all, but there were some four-star performers that she wouldn't mind hooking up with again.

"Let's see." She settled back and smiled as she flipped through the pages. "Three star, three star, two star. Wait. Here we go. Four star—Cedric Daniels— defensive lineman for the Atlanta Falcons. Now that man played a good game between the sheets." The memory of their weekend together a couple years back caused her to start hand-fanning herself. "He would be perfect," she reasoned with herself.

Zora reached for the phone, but then stopped. "Wait—didn't Cedric get married a couple of months ago?" She quickly scrolled through her memory Rolodex and seemed to recall reading something about him marrying some Argentina model in a lavish ceremony. No. She hadn't read about it, Melanie told her about it. She was the one who had introduced him to the girl.

"That had to have been some kind of fluke." Zora shook her head and then planted her nose back into her pink book. "Two star, one star, one star. Oh, here we go. Russell Charles—four stars." Another big smile monopolized Zora's face. She remembered their three-month affair fondly. Russell was a brother who liked to take his time with a woman. He loved mixing things up with toys—food—whatever he could get his hands on. One night, he had her feeling like a banana-split sundae with the whipped cream and chocolate sauce he'd poured all over her body. Of course the fun part was watching and feeling him eat every bit of it off her.

Zora's body quivered deliciously from the old memory.

"Every woman loves a man with a mad head game." She chuckled to herself and again reached for the phone. Once the line was ringing, she sat up with her heart pounding in her throat. What should she say? Would he be happy to hear from her? She was sort of the one to end things between them because of her impossible work schedule.

"Hello."

Zora froze. Could she and should she really go through with this?

"Hello," Russell said again.

"Hey, Russ. Guess who?" The minute the words were out of her mouth, Zora slapped a hand across her forehead. Surely, she could've come up with something better than that.

"Um, I...don't know. How about giving me a hint?"

Zora couldn't tell whether he found the question amusing or annoying so she just cut to the chase. "It's me. Zora."

Silence.

"Zora Campbell," she clarified. She was starting to feel more ridiculous by the second. "We used to—"

"I remember who you are," he finally said, chuckling.

Thank God.

"To what do I owe the pleasure?"

Feeling a little more relaxed, Zora eased back into her chair. "Ah, c'mon now, Russell. You know I've always been fond of you."

"To my recollection, you've always been too busy for me. In the three months that we were together, I had been stood up more times than I care to count. Dating you was a serious blow to my ego."

"I wasn't that bad."

Silence.

Zora tensed up again. "Was I?"

"Zora, you broke my heart. I thought that we really had something going and then…"

The silence was damning. Suddenly, Zora remembered all the times that she had broken dates or forgotten that she was supposed to meet him somewhere. Russell had been great in bed, but outside of it, he was a complete bore. A trust-fund baby himself, Russell never expressed interest in anything outside his privileged upbringing. Though he was generous when he dated women, it didn't escape her notice that he only dated models and actresses. He always had to have something pretty on his arm.

"It doesn't matter," Russell finally finished. "I'm sure we've both moved on. Taylor and I are expecting our first child and no doubt you still have an army of men banging down your door." He laughed.

"Taylor?"

"Yeah, my wife. We're five months along. Of course I would have never met her had it not been for your friend Melanie Harte."

Zora's hand clutched the phone. "Melanie introduced you to your wife?"

"Can you believe it? Me—enlisting the help of a matchmaking service? C'mon, let's face it, I'm not a bad-looking dude—but for some reason I just kept hooking up with the wrong women. Uh, no offense."

Zora rolled her eyes. "None taken."

"Anyway, after you dumped me and I spent a

sufficient amount of time with a new therapist, I let a few of my married friends know that I was back on the prowl. Everyone kept talking about and referring me to the Platinum Society—you know, Melanie's company."

"Yeah, yeah. I'm aware of the name of her company," Zora droned. She was really ready to end this conversation.

"I didn't believe it at first, but the chick really knows her stuff. At least I don't have any complaints," he said.

Yea! Whoopee for you. "Well, I'm glad to hear that, Russ." Zora tried to inject enthusiasm into her voice, but it just didn't work out.

"I'm sorry, I didn't mean to just go on about myself. You hadn't even told me why you were calling." He laughed.

Zora laughed right along with him. She needed a few extra seconds to think of a good lie. "I, um, recently saw Melanie…and um…well, I was like… wow! Russell got married. So I, um, wanted to say congratulations and just—wish you both the best."

"Aww. Well, that's very sweet of you. You know, in retrospect, your breaking up with me was the best thing that ever happened to me. I keep seeing you all over television, pushing this product or that. I gotta tell you—even though it didn't work out with us, I'm very proud and happy for your success."

"Thanks," she deadpanned. "Well, I better go—but good luck to you. Your wife is a lucky woman." After a couple more pleasantries, Zora managed to end the call. When she picked up the pink book again, her exuberance had dropped significantly. This time, she wasn't reading the stars next to anyone's name, but realized that the status for most of these men had changed. "Married, engaged, married, married." She frowned. "When did everybody start getting married?"

Before long, Zora grew disgusted with the whole ordeal and just tossed the pink book across the room. "How pathetic am I if I don't even know how to make a booty call anymore?" Zora moped for a few minutes and then got another idea. In her purse she found a private treasure trove of business cards—all of which had been passed to her from men around the world. Why shouldn't she call a few of them? She didn't need a professional matchmaker to do what she could do herself.

The idea cheered her up. Her love life wasn't DOA just yet. She had plenty of options—and Jaxon Landon wasn't one of them.

"Let me get this straight," Dale said, holding up both hands like stop signs. "You had Zora Campbell crawling on her hands and knees while you stood with your dick out and another chick tryna hitch a ride on the muthafucker?"

Jaxon laughed. "It wasn't *exactly* like that."

"It will be when *I* tell the story." He glanced around the crowded Velvet Rope as if he was going to do just that.

"Will you behave? I have a serious problem on my hands," Jaxon stressed, taking another sip of his drink.

"Aww. C'mon. Where's your sense of humor?" Dale asked, rolling his eyes. "Some of us would be happy to just have one of these hot chicks in this fantasy. You håve the hottest stripper in Manhattan *and* a supermodel and you come up in here whining about it. My only choices are to hate you or wish that I *was* you. But I *certainly* don't pity you."

Jaxon chuckled and shook his head. "I'm not asking for your pity. I'm asking for your help so I can figure out how to fix this."

"What? The big mastermind of Wall Street needs *my* help solving a problem?" Dale set his drink down and then ran his hands through his thinning hair. "Somebody needs to take a picture of this historical moment. Ain't nobody gonna believe this if I tell them."

"All right." Jaxon reached across the table and moved Dale's drink. "I think you've reached your limit for the night."

Dale quickly snatched his drink back. "Hey, I can't think without my go-go juice." He tossed back the remaining contents, signaled a waitress for another and then gave Jaxon his full attention. "All right. So what's the problem?"

"The problem..." Jaxon took his time and drew a deep breath. "Is that I really—really like this woman."

Dale's bushy brows shot up. *"Like?"*

"Well, I just *met* her," Jaxon explained. "But... there was definitely something there. A spark or...something." He relived the moment when he first kneeled at the foot of the gorgeous supermodel and of course the slow journey of his gaze as he traveled up her long, curvaceous body. He couldn't remember ever seeing anything so beautiful. He recalled the sound of blood rushing through his head, his ears felt like they needed popping, and his heart—it felt like it was everywhere: his eyes, his throat, squeezing out of his rib cage. Jaxon had never experienced anything like it. A part of him was telling him that he needed to be scared of a woman who could cause such a wild reaction from him. Another part of him—a stronger part—was both excited and thrilled.

He glanced back up to see Dale staring oddly at him. Jaxon coughed and cleared his throat. "I can't describe it." He looked away.

"Riiight." Dale bobbed his head while he accepted his next drink from the waitress.

Jaxon's defenses kicked in. The last thing he wanted was to appear to be like some starry-eyed, love-struck puppy—even though that was *exactly* how he felt. "Forget it," he said, with a wave. "I'm just trippin'."

"Um, hmm." Dale's stare remained locked on its target.

Jaxon shifted and then pretended to be interested in Tiny, the new girl's awkward dance routine. After a long two minutes, Jaxon could still feel his friend's heavy gaze on him. He cut his eyes back across the table. "What?"

"Man, you know what's what." Dale chuckled. "Damn, I never thought I'd see the day." He shook his head. "Jaxon Landon is in love."

"What? Whoa." Jaxon's hands shot up in the air. "Love? Nobody said anything about all that nonsense. I just said that I liked the girl."

"There was a spark."

"Or something like that," he pressed and then tried to laugh it off. "How in the hell am I in love? I just met the girl."

Dale shrugged. "Hey. Love is fucked up like that. When it happens, it always catches our sorry asses off guard."

Jaxon shook his head. "I like the woman. She's beautiful, captivating and…exciting. I *want* to see her again—*but* none of that means I'm in love."

"So what? You're just looking to hit and quit it? Is that it?"

"Damn. Everything isn't always so black-and-white. There is plenty of room for shades of gray."

"Not when it comes to you." Dale sipped his drink. "At least not as long as I've known you. You either like something or you don't. You either want something or you don't—and you either love someone or you don't."

"Well, I don't," Jaxon clarified.

"But you could."

"Damn. I'm getting dizzy talking to you."

Dale laughed. "The answer to your question is simple."

"Oh, really, Obi-Wan Kenobi? Why don't you enlighten me?"

"If the woman takes the time to build a wall between you, you're going to have to figure a way to lure her out. Find something she wants."

"That's vague."

"C'mon. Everybody wants something or needs something—even a gorgeous supermodel like Zora Campbell. You're just going to have to figure out what that something is. If *anybody* can do that—" Dale cocked his hand like pistol and pretended to fire "—you're the man."

Chapter 8

"We need a better plan," Sylvia declared the moment she entered Melanie's office unannounced. As always, the older woman was immaculately dressed. From her perfectly sculptured silver coif to her polished red nails, Mrs. Landon made it clear that beauty and style didn't have a shelf life. "It's been two weeks and…nothing."

Jessica rushed into Melanie's office with an apology written all over her face.

Melanie stopped her before she uttered a word. "It's all right. Can you close the door on your way out?"

Sylvia glanced over her shoulder at Melanie's embarrassed niece.

"Yes, ma'am." Jessica dropped her head and backtracked out of the office.

Alone, Melanie gestured for Sylvia to have a seat. Once the older woman was settled, Melanie gave her an update. "I wouldn't say that nothing has happened. I have it on good authority from a florist friend of mine that Jaxon has been steadily sending Zora roses every day since they met that night at your anniversary party."

"Really?" Sylvia scooted up to the edge of her chair. A bright beam of hope returned to her eyes. "So he is seeing her?"

"Not exactly," Melanie hedged, taking her time to braid her fingers. "Zora is…a little resistant at the moment. It didn't help that Jaxon's fiancée showed up at the party."

Sylvia rolled her eyes. "Didn't you tell her about the engagement?"

"No. It's not exactly a good selling point when trying to talk someone into a blind date. Plus, I'm not convinced that this engagement is all that it's cracked up to be."

"What do you mean?"

Melanie stood up from behind her desk and moved over to a huge floor-to-ceiling window while she weighed just how much she should say. "I made a few phone calls and did a little studying up on Ms. Kitty Ervin."

"And?" Sylvia was so close to the edge of her

seat that Melanie momentarily feared the older woman was in danger of falling out of it.

"And…no one in her family or at her job seems to be aware of any engagement." Melanie returned to her desk. "And this morning, I had another dear friend of mine return a call regarding that beautiful engagement ring Kitty sported at the party."

"Child, just spit it out. This kind of suspense isn't good on an old lady's heart."

Melanie smiled. "The ring is on loan."

"What?" Sylvia slapped a hand across her mouth and then started laughing her butt off. "I should have known! Jaxon did all of this just to get under our skin." Her laughter deepened. "I bet he thought he was two steps ahead of me. Ha! Well, is the woman even a stripper?"

"She is that. Jaxon is a regular at her establishment—but as far as I can tell, that's about it. In all likelihood, they may have had a minor fling or what-have-you, but nothing that points to it being serious or anything."

"Oh. Thank God!" Sylvia collapsed backward into the chair. "I can't tell you what a relief that is."

"Glad I could help." Melanie returned to her chair. "But my job is far from over."

"You still think that Zora Campbell is the one for him?" Sylvia asked.

"I don't think—I *know* it."

* * *

Clint Blackburn couldn't believe his luck. He was actually out on a date with Zora Campbell. *The* Zora Campbell. The fact challenged any attempt to be calm, cool and collected with the beauty. More than challenged actually, it destroyed it. Two seconds after they'd sat down to dinner at the prestigious Escada's restaurant, he busted out his iPhone and asked the waiter to snap a picture.

"Trust me. None of my boys will believe me if I don't have proof." He laughed.

Zora smiled, but in her mind, she was rolling her eyes. She had hoped for a hot date, but instead felt like she was hosting a radio-contest winner to some fantasy dream date. No doubt this was going to be another evening ending with her curled up in bed with a Sudoku puzzle.

Yippee!

"I have a confession to make," Clint said, leaning forward over the table. "I used to subscribe to *Victoria's Secret* back in college just to see your latest pictures." He cheesed at her. "Not to mention, I had your infamous Miller Lite poster where you wore those cute little blue pasties." He started circling his nipples with his fingers. "You know the one with—"

"Yes. Yes. I remember." Embarrassment burned Zora's cheeks as she glanced around the restaurant, fearful that others were watching her date feel himself up.

"I'm sorry. Sorry," he offered as if realizing he was losing major cool points. "It's just…wow. Zora Campbell." Clint shook his head.

Yes. Yes. I know my name.

"So what made you call me?" he asked. "I mean, I thought I didn't really have a chance in hell when I passed you my card a couple weeks ago. I mean, c'mon. You must have an army of men banging your door down."

"Not exactly an army," she corrected, reaching for a second glass of wine. Clearly, she was going to need a lot of alcohol to get through this evening.

Clint clucked his tongue as he rolled his eyes. "Please. I'm not buying that for a second. But that's cool though. All that matters is that you're out with me tonight, right?"

"Right," she agreed with a convincing smile and another healthy gulp of her pinot grigio. "Sooo. Tell me a little about yourself. What is it that you do for a living? I believe your business card read that you were some kind of consultant?"

"Business consultant," he supplied. "Basically companies call me in to help their employees think outside of the box to become more productive."

That's a job? "Oh, how interesting."

"Well, I have to admit, business is a little a slow— but that's the way it is for everyone right now." He laughed and shook his head. "This economy is hard on a brotha's pockets, knowwhatImean?"

The hackles on the back of Zora's neck stood at attention while a mild panic hit her. The only thing she had in her purse was her driver's license, a folded twenty-dollar bill and a tube of lipstick.

Clint opened the menu and immediately frowned. "Where are the prices on this damn thing?" He laughed again, but it sounded like a misfired weapon—and if she wasn't mistaken there were small beads of sweat lining up along his wrinkled brow.

Zora took another gulp of wine, cleared her throat and then suggested, "If you would like to go somewhere else—?"

"Naw. Naw. I got this." Clint waved off her concern. "I mean, what do I look like taking a super-model to McDonald's?"

"Look, you don't have to try and impress me. If you can't afford—"

"What—what—can't afford this place? Woman, please." Another wave. "I got this. I'm gonna make sure that you have the time of your life tonight."

Zora highly doubted that, but she favored her eager fan with another smile, which waned when the waiter returned and Clint ordered water. It definitely wasn't going to be the time of her life, but she suspected that it was definitely going to be a night she wouldn't forget.

And she was right. The conversation was stilted and one-sided. Clint only wanted to talk about his favorite posters or question her about insane gossip tidbits he'd picked up over the years. Did she ever date this rap star or movie star? Were all famous people on drugs or in rehab? And was her famous ladybug tattoo on the curve of her right ass cheek real or stenciled? It was stenciled.

It was like being interviewed by the *National Enquirer.* For the briefest of moments she could almost understand why someone like Melanie Harte was needed. She could at least weed out the fans and fanatics that wanted nothing more than pictures and autographs in order to brag to their friends. However, she still wasn't willing to give the matchmaker any credit because clearly there was a hiccup in the way she did business.

Setting her up with an engaged man—ha!

The waiter returned for their order and Zora guessed at what would be the cheapest thing on the menu: soup and salad and she turned down another glass of wine for water with a twist of lemon.

"Do they charge for the lemon?" Clint joked.

Zora had a sinking feeling that he was being dead serious. Maybe she needed to sneak to the bathroom and call her assistant to bring her a credit card. Clint ordered the soup, nixed the salad and doubled down on another glass of water—no lemon.

The moment the waiter walked off, Zora tried again to get the man to reconsider McDonald's. Hell, she wasn't trying to break the man.

"Please, girl. I told you I had this." He winked at her and then tried to wipe his brow on the sly. There were other visible signs of distress, as well. He kept bouncing his leg to the point it started shaking the table—and he seemed unable to make the decision whether to lay his napkin on his lap or tuck it into his collar.

When their sparse food arrived, Zora's stomach felt as if it was rumbling in protest for the lack of protein on the plate. Other models may try to survive on nothing, but she certainly wasn't one of them.

"I know one thing," Clint said, still trying to lighten the mood. "This better be some damn good soup or this shit is going back." His strange laugh was now grating on Zora's last nerve.

Just finish dinner and then hop in the first cab you see to go home.

"You know, I was thinking that after dinner, I could show you how the other half lives."

Zora frowned. "What half is that?"

"You know. Us middle-class brothas down in the Bronx." He cheesed some more. "I'll take you down to my place. We can cuddle up on my new sofa. I got this great deal at IKEA."

Zora suddenly had a piercing headache. "Um, I don't know. I have a really full day tomorrow—"

"Don't worry. I got a new bed, too. You're more than welcome to crash on it if you need to."

Zora choked on a piece of lettuce.

Clint was instantly on her and pounding her back. He damn near snapped it in half. "You aight?"

She frantically nodded and waved him off. It was either that or spend the rest of her life in a wheelchair. When Clint stopped, she excused herself to tend to all the tears racing down her face and possibly ruining her makeup. "Excuse me." She hopped up and ran off.

"All right. Don't stay away too long. I hate to think you'd walk out on me and this check."

Zora's entire body heated with embarrassment when half the patrons' heads swiveled in her direction. In the bathroom, she quickly punched in her assistant's phone number and prayed.

But apparently God was too busy solving world peace or something because Monica was off pretending like she actually had a life outside her job and wasn't answering her phone. When her voice mail finally came on, Zora made her desperate plea. "Monica, Monica, please. I need you to call me back. I'm on the date from hell, I need you to bring me some money because I think I'm about to get stuck with the bill. Please. Please. Call me back as soon as you get this message. *Please!*" Zora disconnected the phone and waited a few minutes, still hoping against hope that Monica would immediately call her back.

Again, her prayers weren't being patched

through God's direct line so she slinked over to the large vanity mirror and fixed her eye makeup. More time passed and it became clear that Monica wasn't going to rescue her anytime soon. That meant it was time to put on her big-girl panties and go back out there and face the music.

Zora exited the bathroom and as she made her way back through the restaurant, she felt like a dead woman walking.

"There you are, girl. I was just about to ask one of the waitresses to go and check in on you."

"I'm good," she said and returned to her seat. She was as nervous about the check as he looked. As a way to stall, she and Clint made weak attempts to turn meaningless chatter into deep conversation. Inevitably the bill arrived and both Zora and Clint fell silent and stared at the leather folder as if by doing that, the bill would magically disappear.

Ten looong minutes later, the waiter returned to see if they needed anything else—both knew that it was a subtle hint for a credit card.

"Um, yeah. I think I'd like some more water," Clint stalled.

"Yes, sir." The waiter disappeared again.

While he was gone, Clint finally worked up the nerve to peek at the check. "A hundred and fifty-six dollars?" he thundered and then glanced around their table. "You gotta be kidding me. For one salad and two bowls of soup?"

"I did have two glasses of wine," Zora meekly reminded him and then felt guilty when fear blanketed his face. "Look, if you can't—"

"Hey, hey." Clint held up his hands as full stop signs. "I said I had this, baby girl. So let me do what I do." He reached into his jacket and finally removed his wallet—complete with a Velcro latch—and removed his VISA card.

The waiter, like an eagle swooping in on its prey, grabbed the bill and the credit card before Clint had a chance to process what had happened. When he finally did, he looked like he was ready to start crying. There was nothing to do but to wait it out.

Turned out—they didn't have to wait long.

"I'm sorry, sir—but your card has been declined."

"What?"

Oh, God. Zora sank down into her seat.

"Perhaps you have another card?" the waiter suggested.

"I don't need another card. Ain't nothing wrong with that one." Clint pushed the card back toward the waiter. "Try it again. I know there's money in that account. I just deposited two hundred dollars in that bad boy this morning."

"Sir—"

"I said, run it again."

Forget God saving her, Zora would settle for the devil opening the floor and swallowing her up.

"I tell you what," the waiter said, his smile still

firmly in place. "Why don't I let you talk to the manager?" He set Clint's card back down in front of him.

"Yeah. You do that," Clint mocked, puffing out his chest. "I'd love to give him a piece of my mind about this ridiculously overpriced establishment."

"As you wish." The waiter pivoted and then marched like a solider off to war.

Once he was gone, Zora couldn't help but hiss, "What the hell do you think you're doing?"

"What? I got this," he continued to insist.

"Who in the hell do you think you're kidding?" She removed the napkin from her lap and slapped it onto the table. "You're not fooling anyone. You don't have enough money to cover the bill on your *debit* card. Why didn't we leave when we had a chance to?"

"Oh, because I have a *debit card* instead a real VISA card, I ain't good enough for you?"

"What?"

"Uh-huh. Hell, I don't know why I'm the one footing the bill in the first place. You were the one who asked *me* out. You were the one who picked this bougie-ass place where they're charging, like, fifty damn dollars for a glass of water."

Flabbergasted, Zora's mouth fell open. This was *her* fault?

"You know what?" He hopped out of his chair. "I'ma bounce."

"What?"

"It's been real." He tipped his head and then he was gone.

Zora was too stunned to do anything other than to watch him go. Surprisingly, she was relieved. So much so that it was worth the very real possibility of management calling the police on her when they learned that she didn't have the money to pay for their bill.

Then she felt it—that familiar magnetic pull that created and caused invisible butterflies to flutter wildly in the pit of her stomach. For a few quickened heartbeats, she was afraid to turn and look, but the pull proved to be too strong and her neck slowly turned until her gaze crashed into Jaxon Landon.

And horror of all horrors, he was making his way to her table.

Chapter 9

Jaxon felt like the luckiest sonofabitch in New York.

He'd spent the whole day looking and hoping to stumble across some information that would lure his beautiful supermodel out of her ice castle and here the opportunity of a lifetime just fell into his lap. He even enjoyed the panicked look on his prey as he approached the table. Despite being a seasoned poker player, he couldn't fight back the smile that crept across his face.

"Hello, Ms. Campbell," he greeted, pulling out a chair and making himself comfortable. "I hear that we have ourselves a problem."

"You can't be the manager," she said dubiously.

"No," he admitted with a shrug. "I'm just the owner—well, co-owner. Will that do?"

Zora shifted in her seat, glanced around the restaurant and noticed just a couple heads turned in their direction so she leaned forward and tried to whisper. "Look, there has been this huge misunderstanding tonight. My date, um, was…a little bit short and—"

"Ah, yes. Your date." Jaxon also glanced around. "Seems like you picked a real winner. Meanwhile, my flowers and phone calls are ignored. I don't want to say that my ego is bruised, *but* it might be."

"Look. I'm not interested in you or your big ego."

"Ah. You do remember it was big."

Embarrassed, Zora's eyes widened and blinking became a challenge. "I didn't say— I wasn't referring—"

Jaxon's smile turned downright sinister. "If it helps, you made quite an impression on me, too. I'm just sorry that we never got that chance to talk in my grandparents' library. I think a lot of the…*misunderstandings* between us could have been resolved."

"Misunderstandings?" Laughing, Zora folded her arms and leaned back in her chair. "First of all, there isn't anything *between* us and the second thing is there's been no misunderstanding. You're engaged and I don't *date* other women's men. Call me picky." She flashed him a quick, fake smile and then leveled him with an icy stare. If she'd hoped to shave a few inches off his smug smile, she failed miserably. Instead, the unflappably cool ladies' man looked more amused than turned off.

"Has anyone ever told you that you're a beautiful but lousy liar?"

Zora sucked in a startled breath.

"There is *definitely* something between us." To prove his point, he reached across the table and lightly brushed his hand across her arm.

Despite the instant electric charge that caused the tiny hairs along her arm to stand, Zora didn't jerk back. For some strange reason, she couldn't. In fact, his touch activated a switch that had her imagination conjuring realistic images and sensations of what it would feel like if Jaxon ran his hands on different parts of her body. Instantly, she started quivering and shivering with phantom orgasms that caused her face to darken to a deep cranberry.

Jaxon arched an inquisitive brow, but before he could question her, she finally pulled her arm from his troubling touch. "Looks like it was good for you, too."

Zora coughed to clear her throat, but when she tried to speak again, it sounded as if she still had a two-hundred-pound frog blocking her airways.

"I'm sorry. I didn't catch that," Jaxon said, cupping his ear and leaning closer.

Zora coughed harder and then tested her voice with a small hum before talking. "Mr. Landon, if—"

"Oh, are we back to being formal? I'd hoped that

we were at least friends by now—seeing how you saw me naked and everything—well, a part of me naked anyway."

Zora's face passed cranberry and was quickly approaching the color of eggplant.

"Of course, I wished the opportunity had been under different circumstances and say, there were less people around. Unless you're into that sort of thing, then maybe—"

"Stop. Stop." Zora held up her hands, wanting this cat and mouse game to end. "Let's just discuss the matter at hand. I don't have the money for the bill, but I'm good for it. If I can just go home and grab a credit card, I'll come back and take care of everything. I promise. I'm good for it."

Jaxon sat there, stared.

"Well?" she prompted, hoping she could hurry up and end this nightmare of an evening sooner rather than later.

"Well, what?" Jaxon asked.

"Can I leave and bring you back a credit card? You know who I am. It's not like I'm—"

"Oh, you'd like special treatment because you're a celebrity." Jaxon rolled his eyes. "Typical."

"What?" Zora glanced around again. Her paranoia convinced her that there were a few more heads turned in her direction than the last time. "That was not what I meant, and *you* know it."

Jaxon gave her a careless half shrug. "I know

nothing of the kind. I mean, I've only met you once, *Ms. Campbell*—and you did sort of stand me up for the library. Come to find out that you're really not a friend of my grandparents. All evidence points to you crashing their anniversary party—though I can't imagine why. Surely you are invited to more happening parties."

"I had a date."

"Oh?" He laughed. "The same one that bailed and stiffed you with tonight's tab or are we talking about a different asshole?"

Zora laughed. "Definitely a different asshole."

"Like those, do you?"

She jumped to her feet. "I'm out of here." She snatched up her purse. "For the record, you have to be the most arrogant, insufferable asshole I've ever met. As far as your *big* ego—I've seen *bigger!*" She took one step and Jaxon's hand shot out like a python strike and stopped Zora in her tracks.

"I didn't say that you could go."

Zora couldn't believe her ears. "I don't need your permission."

"Actually—" Jaxon stood and towered over her "—you do. Unless you want to explain your skipping out on your bill to the police…and whatever tabloid I happen to dial up."

"You wouldn't," she hissed.

"I would—and you know it."

There was no doubt in Zora's mind that everyone in the restaurant was now looking at them, while her eyes locked in a silent battle with Jaxon. Zora knew within seconds, it was a war that she wasn't going to win.

"Better yet," he said suddenly. "Let's continue this conversation in one of the wine rooms." Jaxon snapped his fingers and the next thing Zora knew they were being ushered to a private room in the back of the restaurant.

The whole time, Zora's heart pounded so hard and loud that it drowned out her thoughts—or maybe the truth was that she wasn't thinking at all. She was just…feeling. She couldn't remember the last time she'd ever felt anything remotely close to what she was feeling now. It was a heady combination of anxiousness, excitement and fear all rolled into one. It made her light-headed, weak-kneed and still she followed.

I can stop now and turn around, she reasoned. She didn't stop walking until she was at the private room's archway. Only then did some semblance of sanity trickle through her mind, but by then it was too late.

"Come in," Jaxon beckoned in that same buttery baritone that could seduce a nun.

Zora stepped in from the marble hallway onto an exotic Oriental rug.

Jaxon stood by the fireplace, while a new fire

crackled to life. The wine room was dim to the point of being romantic.

"How come I get the feeling this isn't the first time you've invited a woman back here?"

Jaxon cocked a half smile, but didn't take the bait. "Would you like a drink?"

"Sure. Why not?"

He nodded and then moved across the room toward a handsome mahogany bar. "Have a seat," he instructed.

Amazingly, she continued to follow orders. She took a spot on a leather chaise adjacent to the fire-place.

Jaxon adjusted his jacket. "Now. See? That wasn't so hard, was it? What would you like?" He set two glasses down on the bar and then plopped two ice cubes in each one.

Zora tilted her head. "What the hell do you think you're doing?"

"Don't worry. I can afford *my* tab." He winked. "What'll it be?"

"Surprise me."

He smiled. "A woman who's not afraid to take risks," he concluded. "Means you're a woman after my own heart," he added.

Why did that simple praise make her feel giddy? "Okay, moneybags. Then you can loan me the money for my tab and I can pay you back tomorrow."

"Oh, no." He playfully held up his hands and shook his head. "I don't like loaning money. It makes things sticky between friends. I mean, if you can't pay me back then the next thing you know I have to play bill collector. Then you would start avoiding my calls and pretending that you don't remember borrowing any money. Loaning money is a messy business."

"It's just a hundred and fifty-six dollars."

"Which apparently *you* don't have right now."

"I…" Zora snapped her mouth shut when the waiter returned.

"Is there anything else I can get you, sir?"

Jaxon smiled. "No. We're good."

When they were alone again, Jaxon offered up his glass for a toast.

"And just what the hell are we toasting to?"

"To new beginnings, of course." He tapped his glass against hers and took his first sip without waiting for her response.

At this point, Zora needed this drink. It was probably the only thing that could steady her nerves. She meant to only take a sip, but the moment the glass pressed against her lips, she gulped down the whole contents as if it was water.

"Thirsty?" Jaxon asked, amused.

"More like annoyed."

He pressed a hand against his chest. "With me?" He actually managed to pull off a confused and hurt look. "Excuse me, but I don't believe that *I* was the one who took you out to dinner and then stiffed you with the bill."

"No. You're just the one that's holding me hostage until…"

Jaxon's eyebrows jumped. "Until?"

Zora set her glass down and crossed her arms. "Until you get something out of me."

"Um. You mean like a tit-for-tat sort of thing?" Jaxon leaned forward, placed both elbows on the table while he stroked an invisible goatee. "That would be pretty immature of me," he concurred as if she were presenting the idea. "But what do you think would be a fair exchange for something like this?"

"Oh, please. Don't try and play me."

"No. No." He straightened in his chair in an attempt to put his best foot forward. "I like where you were going with this. When you think about it, I'd be taking one heck of a chance on you actually returning to pay your bill. I mean, you should be good for it—but you never know. One reads all the time about how you celebrity types have a hard time managing your money."

"Then I'll sign a promissory note," she said, frustrated.

"You mean like a check? Oh, well. Why didn't you say so? We'll make an exception and take a check. You have your checkbook?"

Zora clamped her jaw shut and proceeded to grind her back teeth.

"I'm going to take that as a *no*." He clucked his tongue and shook his head. "You got yourself in quite a predicament here. And I have to say that I'm a bit disappointed in you."

"What?"

"I know I'm technically batting for the other side, but I would've thought that a dating veteran—such as yourself—would have a contingency plan for such situations like this. There are a lot of assholes out here. I know. I'm one of them."

"Glad you can admit it." Zora shifted in her chair and eyeballed her empty glass.

Jaxon poured her another. "You might look like a lightweight, but something tells me that you could drink me under the table."

"Are you challenging me? Maybe want to make a wager—say, for one hundred and fifty-six dollars?"

His eyes lit up. The bet surprised—and tempted him. "Something tells me it wouldn't be a wise wager on my part."

"Meaning, you're afraid that you'll lose?"

"I *never* lose—because I don't take unnecessary risks."

Zora rolled her eyes. "Whatever. Chicken."

"Sticks and stones." He chuckled and then went back to staring at her. "You didn't bring *any* money with you?"

She shrugged. "I have twenty dollars for a cab—okay?"

Jaxon sucked in a breath. "Twenty dollars? Where do you live—around the block?"

"Wouldn't you like to know?"

"I already know. It was a rhetorical question." He waved off her irritation with a flip of his wrist. "Refill?" Again, he didn't wait for an answer, he just started pouring.

Zora didn't stop him, but the voice in the back of her head told her to slow down. Clearly, she was going to need her wits about her when dealing with Jaxon. "Do me a favor and just spit it out," she said.

"Spit what out?"

She rolled her eyes at his determination to play dumb. "Whatever it is that you want."

He opened his mouth to argue, but she quickly cut him off. "Don't insult my intelligence by pretending not to know what I'm talking about. You want something from me in order to make this one-hundred-dollar problem go away."

"A hundred and *fifty-six* dollars," he corrected.

"What is it?"

Their eyes locked again while they both put up one hell of a fight against the unexplainable and undeniable magnetic pull flowing between them.

"A date," he finally said. "One whole evening alone with me—tomorrow night."

Zora's eyes narrowed. "Tomorrow?"

"We go where I choose—for as long as I choose. There will be no backing out, rain checks or excuses of any kind."

"Will your fiancée be joining us on this date?"

Jaxon laughed. "Well, *that* didn't take long, now did it?"

"That's not an answer," she pressed. There was a small part of her fighting not to be completely charmed by this handsome devil—at least not yet.

"It's sort of complicated," he admitted, studying her.

"I'm a smart girl. I'm sure I'll be able to follow whatever bullshit explanation you come up with."

He now wore a full smile that seemed to evaporate all the oxygen in the air. Of course it didn't help that the soft amber glow from the fire seemed to dance off his caramel skin. Everything about him just *seemed* to be too good to be true.

"Can you keep a secret?" Jaxon asked, serious.

The question surprised Zora, but then she nodded and waited.

After a couple of silent seconds, Jaxon confessed. "Kitty is not *really* my fiancée."

"Oh, really?" She kept her voice neutral, but she had a hard time swallowing that pill. "So you usually put a rock that big on a woman's hand for—what—shits and giggles?"

"Usually? No. Though it's a nice ring. It's on loan to me from a friend of mine at Cartier."

"Riiight." Zora's instincts were to laugh. "Surely, you're pulling my leg?"

"No. But I could, if you like. If memory serves me correct, you have the best pair of legs in the business. Taut, long and curvy." His eyes locked on hers. "Another secret. I'm definitely a leg man."

Zora frowned. She didn't know how to take this information. She certainly didn't think she should believe him. "All right. Why on earth do you have a fake fiancée?"

"Like I said. It's a little complicated." He tilted up his drink.

"Like *I* said, I'm a smart girl."

He hit her with another smile that made her light-headed. "And beautiful."

Zora had had millions tell her that, but none of them ever came even close to making her blush the way she was right now. "Thank you."

"The question is," he went on, "what am I going to do with you?"

That threw her off. Of course he was making a habit of doing that. "I'm not quite sure that there is something to be done with me," she volleyed.

"Oooh. I wouldn't go that far," he said, taking another sip of his drink. "I can think of a million things to do with you. I just don't know which one I want to do *first*." Jaxon watched her over the rim of his glass. "Then again I'm making a lot of pre-sumptions," he said.

"Especially for one hundred and fifty-six dollars." Zora coughed to try to shove her heart back down into her chest.

"Do *you* have a man, Zora?"

It was another zinger, taking her off guard. "You know I don't."

"Would you like one?"

Zora's mouth moved but words eluded her.

Jaxon lifted a single groomed brow. "Need to think about it?"

Zora closed her eyes, which gave her the chance to collect herself. When she finally opened them again, she was laughing. "I have to hand it to you, Mr. Landon. You *are* smooth." She tossed back her drink, but this time it burned down the wrong pipe. She started coughing and then hacking.

"Whoa, there." Jaxon eased next to her on the chaise and lightly patted her on the back. "I take it you're not a bourbon girl."

The only problem was his proximity only robbed her of more oxygen so her hacking turned into a full-fledged choking fit.

Jaxon took the glass from her hand and set it aside. "Put your hands up over your head."

In no position to argue, Zora shot her hands high into the air while Jaxon slapped her back just a little more forcefully. She had no doubts that she had turned a new shade of purple for a moment. It was probably about the time she started seeing white spots dance before her eyes. Luckily, a couple seconds later, her lungs finally accepted oxygen and started dragging it in for the lifesaving sustenance that it was.

"There you go. Now deep breaths," Jaxon coached.

When it was all over with, there were fat tears rolling down her face and probably doing quite a number on her makeup and Jaxon's black gaze was locked on her heaving chest. She bolted up from the chair. This had gone on for too long. "I better go."

"We haven't finished striking our deal," he said too calmly. "There's no need to run. I don't bite… hard."

Zora stopped and faced him. "I need to get home…and you need to get back to your *fiancée*."

Jaxon stood and the room shrank. "I told you. She's not my fiancée."

"Oooh. Right. I forgot," Zora said, rolling her eyes.

Jaxon's smile disappeared. "You'll learn, Ms. Campbell, that I am many things—but I am *not* a liar."

"Sure you are," Zora said smugly. "Either you're lying now or you lied to every single person at your grandparents' party. Which is it?"

Jaxon's brows jumped and then the restaurant was suddenly filled with his rich, melodious, baritone laughter. "You know, I really hadn't thought about it like that."

"How *did* you think of it?"

"As a practical joke to get my grandparents off my ass about settling down and turning one of their selected trust-fund debutantes into a baby-factory machine for two years until we divorce and I'm strapped into paying an outrageous sum of money for child support and alimony."

The handsome devil was full of surprises.

"Silly, I know," he conceded. "I was just looking to buy myself a little break from their constant hounding. Everything was going along swimmingly—until you showed up that night."

"Your grandmother?" A light went off in Zora's head. The pieces of the puzzle were snapping together at lightning speed—especially Melanie's part in all this. If Jaxon didn't hire Melanie, then it stood to reason that perhaps his meddlesome grandmother had.

Next thing Zora knew, she was laughing again. However, after she went on for a full minute, Jaxon started looking at her as if wondering whether she was playing with a full deck. She started to explain herself, but then remembered her promise to Melanie. So instead, she just said, "I believe you."

"Good," he said, pleased. "Can I fix you another drink?"

"I don't know about that," she conceded, shaking her head. Just because she had figured out the moving pieces to this puzzle didn't mean that she had arrived at any decisions about the man before her. "I, um…"

Jaxon cocked his head. "Do I make you nervous, Ms. Campbell?"

Deny. Deny. Deny. "A little."

That half smile that she was starting to adore tilted his lips. "Then what can I do to relax you?"

Zora nearly fainted at the possibilities.

He smiled as if he'd just read her private thoughts. "I've never said this to another woman before, but Ms. Campbell, you simply fascinate me." His eyes tenderly roamed from the top her head to her painted toes. "Absolutely and completely."

She could easily say the same about him. He was a walking, talking fantasy that was causing her body to tingle and throb all over.

Jaxon's eyes traveled back up to her face. His gaze focused on her full lips. "I wonder," he whispered.

Zora swallowed and then whispered back, "Wonder what?"

"If you taste as good as you look."

Cocking her own confident smile, she answered, "Better."

He laughed. "We have a date?"

Laughing, she prayed that she wouldn't regret what she was about to do. "All right." She stared into his hypnotic eyes. "We have a date."

"Good. Now just one more thing—I'd like to give you a ride home tonight."

Chapter 10

"You owe me, big-time," Clint Blackburn said, pouting from the back of Melanie's black limousine. "I still can't believe that I just threw away the chance of a lifetime with *the* Zora Campbell." He smacked a hand across his forehead. "Stupid, stupid, stupid."

"Oh, stop being melodramatic," Melanie said, pulling her BlackBerry out of her purse. "It would have never worked between you two. Besides. I have the perfect woman in mind for you. Trust me on this." She answered the ringing phone while Clint cast a dubious look.

Hell, it was too late now. Zora would forever think he was a lowlife that stiffed her with the check in one of Manhattan's überelite restaurants. His stomach hadn't stopped twisting into knots since Melanie first laid out tonight's plan.

"Hello, Jamie? How's it going in there?"

Clint frowned when he recognized the name. "You even had our waiter involved in this mess?"

"Shhh." Melanie waved him off, and then in the next second, a huge smile monopolized her face. "Oooh, reeaally? They're in a private room?" She turned toward Clint with her hand held up for a high five.

He didn't give her one.

She covered a hand over the mouthpiece. "Don't be a spoilsport. I told you, I'll hook you up. Trust me. I'm one of the best in the business."

"It's a little scary seeing how you operate behind the curtain."

"All that matters is that I have a ninety-five percent success rate—and I'm not about to let a silly little thing like a fake engagement set me back."

"What?"

"Never mind." She waved him off again and then returned her attention to the phone. "Thanks, Jamie. Keep me posted." She disconnected the call and quickly dialed a number. "Hello, Sylvia. We got them. Hook, line and sinker."

"A ride home?" Zora asked, wide-eyed.

"As a part of our deal," he added, licking his

lower lip and staring at her as if she was a five-course meal on Thanksgiving Day.

"I don't…"

"Now look who's chicken," he taunted. "What the heck do you think I'm going to do—kidnap you?" He sat down next to her. "Maybe tie you up and have my way with you?"

That two-hundred-pound frog squeezed back into the middle of her throat and this time threatened to choke the daylights out of her.

"I mean, I could—if that's the sort of thing you're into." He winked.

Zora slammed her eyes shut to break the trance she'd fallen under, but not in time to stop another miniorgasm from coursing down her spine and exploding at the tip of her clit. When she opened her eyes again, he stood so close to her face that his warm breath caressed her like a lover's touch.

"It's just a simple ride." He cocked his head and his lips came so close to hers that she sighed aloud.

Jaxon smiled. "I'm going to take that as a *yes*." Then, as if he couldn't control himself any longer, his head descended and his warm, hungry mouth ravished hers in a kiss she knew she would remember for the rest of her life.

He tasted like spearmint and bourbon and his tongue performed this erotic dance inside her mouth that instantly made Zora wet. Next thing she knew, her body was smashed against his hard frame.

Again, she thought she would faint, this time from the feel of the wonderfully hard ridges of this black god's body. There didn't seem to be a soft spot on him. Zora had spent a lifetime knowing and working her body in front of a camera. This was the first time in memory that she didn't have control over what she was doing or feeling. The more she drank from his lips the more she wanted.

This can't be happening. This can't be happening.

But it was happening. Right there in a private wine room in the back of a restaurant. And to make matters worse, her horny body had shut off all pathways for her brain to do anything about what was going on. Her body wanted this, craved this, and by hell or high water, it was going to get it.

Served her right for psyching herself up for two days to make a booty call.

"Damn, you *do* taste good," he whispered and then planted his hot mouth against the column of her neck, where she giggled and quivered. Yet at the same time, she clung to him like he was the last life preserver on the Titanic.

Jaxon's head swam. He just meant to steal one little kiss, but the moment his lips made contact, his head went into another zone. Somehow he was falling and flying at the same time. Next, he was sinking his fingers through her hair, then down her long back and around her firm, tight ass.

Comfortable in the role of being the aggressor,

he gave it a good squeeze and then swallowed her responsive gasp greedily.

Slow it down. You'll scare her away.

However, reason had a hard time penetrating his—admittedly—thick skull. She just tasted and felt too good to be true. He leaned her back, stretched her out over the thick, upholstered chaise while his hands roamed over her famous curves.

I'll stop in a minute, quickly turned into *I'll stop, if she tells me to*—then finally, *Please, don't tell me to stop.*

Please.

Don't.

Zora couldn't breathe. At least, that was what it felt like. She was hot, dizzy and losing the fight against insanity. Especially now that she could feel Jaxon's strong fingers creeping up the inside of her thighs. *We shouldn't.*

She tried to gasp for oxygen; instead she felt as if she'd inhaled some kind of drug for all the help that it had done her. One finger brushed along the seat of her panties and she damn near came unglued. Her nails sank into the hard muscles along his broad back and she heard a long steady hiss escape from Jaxon's clenched teeth—but he didn't stop.

I can't.

Two fingers ran against the bottom of her panties and then circled around her throbbing clit. Automatically, her hips soared upward and when they came back down, Jaxon had shoved the damp material over to the corner of her thigh so that her exposed wet clit mopped the pads of his finger.

"Sssssh," she gasped.

"Damn. You even feel good, too," he praised.

Zora Michelle Campbell, you stop this—right now!

"Sssssh," she responded to her badgering inner voice when his index finger started making lazy figure eights inside her.

"Aww. Yes, baby," Jaxon whispered. "You've been wanting this from the moment we laid eyes on each other, haven't you?"

No! No!

She opened her mouth to talk, but all she could manage was a long moan and a couple of whimpers.

"You just like giving a brother a hard time, don't you?" His fingers sped up, slowed down and sped up again. "You just like playing hard to get, don't you, baby?"

Zora tried to listen, but that small inner voice grew further and further away. It didn't matter that she was in the back of an exclusive restaurant with a man she couldn't stand just a couple of hours ago, but was now on the verge of an orgasm. It was cheap and she didn't even want to review what had led her to this point. That would come much later. Right now, she just wanted and needed this building orgasm more than she needed something as overrated as oxygen.

"Oh, shit," she gasped.

Jaxon blinked in surprise. She was such a pretty thing with a dirty mouth.

"Fuck. I'm coming." Zora started inching up the curvy chaise, her eyes wide and locked on the man in front of her.

Jaxon matched her bold stare with one of his own and drank in the vivid emotions that played across her face. As her orgasm crested, her mouth slowly sagged open and her upper lip quivered. Then—*Bam!*

"Ahhh!" Instantly, her legs sprang closed and her knees tried to lock together.

Jaxon couldn't help but laugh as he struggled to pull his hand out from her thighs' death grip.

Big mistake, because all Zora heard and understood was that he was laughing at her. She sprang to her feet, shoved her dress back down her waist and bolted toward the door.

"Zora, wait!"

She took off, oblivious that she looked like a disheveled mess as she rushed through the restaurant like a three-alarm fire.

Jaxon was right on her heels, but conscious enough to smile and give reassuring nods to his eating patrons as he went. Of course he still probably looked ridiculous carrying a woman's clutch purse, but he was determined to make it work.

The moment Zora stepped out onto the sidewalk, her hand shot high into the air. "Taxi!"

* * *

From across the street, Melanie Harte's head shot up from the extensive questionnaire she was filling out with Clint Blackburn. She even had a DVD playing introducing new clients to the Platinum Society when she glanced out of the limo's dark tinted windows in time to see a yellow cab practically screech to a halt in front of the restaurant.

"What the hell?"

"Zora, wait!" Jaxon yelled, racing out the restaurant. He didn't make it to the cab before it peeled away with a cloud of smoke jetting from its tailpipe.

Melanie slumped back against her seat. "That doesn't look good." Her phone rang. It was Jamie, the waiter. "Yeah. Yeah. I saw. Thanks." She disconnected the call as she watched Jaxon swear and kick at the curb.

"Looks like this one is going to fall into that little five-percent failure column," Clint said smugly.

Melanie grounded her teeth together and did a little mental swearing herself. But she refused to believe that she was wrong about Zora and Jaxon. She just had to figure out a way to make her see what she already knew: they were perfect for each other—damn it!

An Important Message from the Publisher

Dear Reader,

Because you've chosen to read one of our fine novels, I'd like to say "thank you"! And, as a special way to say thank you, I'm offering to send you two more Kimani™ Romance novels and two surprise gifts— absolutely FREE! These books will keep it real with true-to-life African American characters that turn up the heat and sizzle with passion.

Please enjoy the free books and gifts with our compliments...

Glenda Howard

For Kimani Press

Peel off Seal and Place Inside...

(K-ROM-10R2)

W e'd like to send you two free books to introduce you to Kimani™ Romance books. These novels feature strong, sexy women, and African-American heroes that are charming, loving and true. Our authors fill each page with exceptional dialogue, exciting plot twists, and enough sizzling romance to keep you riveted until the very end!

KIMANI ROMANCE...LOVE'S ULTIMATE DESTINATION

Your two books have a combined cover price of $13.98, but are yours **FREE!**

We'll even send you two wonderful surprise gifts. You can't lose!

BUSINESS REPLY MAIL
FIRST-CLASS MAIL   PERMIT NO. 717   BUFFALO, NY

POSTAGE WILL BE PAID BY ADDRESSEE

THE READER SERVICE
PO BOX 1867
BUFFALO NY 14240-9952

NO POSTAGE
NECESSARY
IF MAILED
IN THE
UNITED STATES

Chapter 11

Zora was embarrassed—no—mortified. No matter how hard she tried to review exactly what happened tonight, she couldn't come up with a single plausible answer to how the hell she'd lost her mind. And she had most certainly lost it.

"Where are we going, lady?" the cab driver asked.

Jarred out of her scrambling thoughts, Zora's eyes jumped to the rearview mirror where she met the driver's gaze. "Um, the Time Warner Center at Columbus Circle," she answered.

"Heeey, don't I know you?" he asked, squinting. "Yeah, yeah. You're that sexy model, um." He snapped his fingers. "Zora Campbell!"

Zora smiled while she raked her fingers through her tousled hair.

"Wow," the driver went on. "Who was that chasing you out of the restaurant—your boyfriend?"

"N-no. Not exactly." She cleared her throat and glanced out of the side window.

"Oh. Why—did you two have an argument or something?"

Zora clammed up. Why did people assume that they were entitled to know all her business just because they knew her name?

"Ah. Don't worry. I'm not the kind of person that'll blab to the tabloids. Hassan hears no evil, sees no evil and speaks no evil." He pretended to zip his lips. "Trust me. In this job, it's best to keep your mouth shut. You know what I mean?"

Zora didn't answer.

"Yeah, I see famous people all the time. How can I not? This is Manhattan—home to thousands of celebrities. Like this morning. Who gets into my cab other than—Robert De Niro. *The* Robert De Niro. You can't imagine what it's like to get the most famous *Taxi Driver* into your cab." The man's face exploded into a smile. "I mean, c'mon. *De Niro.* You know, 'Are you talkin' to me?'" He laughed. "Aw, man, I must've done my impersonation of him for like twenty minutes. He loved it."

Zora tuned out the chatty cab driver so she could

again replay tonight's fiasco back in her mind. Maybe she'd had too much to drink. But that couldn't have been true because she was definitely sober now. She nibbled on her bottom lip. She could only imagine what Jaxon Landon thought of her.

Crazy.

Pathetic.

Easy.

Desperate.

The sad part was that every one of those adjectives had a snippet of truth to them. While she was now trying to act all indignant, she had called and arranged this evening with the full intent of getting laid—with a handsome loser who skipped out on the check. Maybe she did need help in the dating arena because clearly she didn't have a clue to what she was doing.

"Annnd here we are," Hassan announced. "The Time Warner Building." He tried to glance up at the building. "Pretty fancy digs."

"Thank you. How much do I owe you?" She reached for her purse only to find the seat next to her empty.

"Thirty-six seventy-five—but you can just pay me thirty-six dollars." He smiled.

"Oh, God, I don't believe this!" Zora started searching around.

"Problem?"

"Hassan, tonight has been nothing but one *big* problem."

* * *

"Sooo, you're *not* engaged," Carlton asked, making sure that he was keeping up with his grandson's explanation.

"No," Jaxon answered simply and then castled his king on the marble chessboard. Even after making the move, he questioned whether he'd made the right one.

With hardly a glance at the board, Carlton reached over and made his own move. "Check."

Jaxon clamped his jaw tight and started to grind his back molars. How in the hell did he miss that move?

"Okay," Carlton said, staring at Jaxon from across the table. "Mind if I ask why you would fake an engagement—or is that sticking my nose where it doesn't belong again?"

The conversation was quickly becoming an unwanted distraction. As usual Jaxon tried to concentrate 200 percent on beating his grandfather—a feat that he had never managed to accomplish. Hell, at this point in his life, he would be happy to just achieve a stalemate compared to the all-out ass-whooping Carlton usually gave him on the board.

"Jaxon?" Carlton probed.

"Um? Oh, it was just a practical joke that got out of hand," he admitted without pulling his gaze from the board. "I know I was wrong and I'm sorry for not coming clean sooner."

Carlton was quiet for a long time. But long stretches of silence weren't uncommon between them so Jaxon continued to contemplate his next move.

"Son," he started.

Jaxon's gaze shot up. "I've asked you not to call me that." As intended, Carlton appeared rebuffed by Jaxon's tone. In the next second, Jaxon regretted snapping.

Carlton tried again. "I just find it a little disappointing that you felt that you needed to go to such extremes to…"

"To what?" Jaxon challenged. "To get both of you off my back?"

"We weren't trying to—"

"Please." Jaxon pushed away from the table and stood. "Let's not kid each other. Nothing I do is ever good enough in this family."

"What—you need a constant pat on the back?" Carlton thundered. His blue eyes were bright with disappointment. "It's not my job to stand here and coddle you. I did all I could to toughen you up—prepare you for the sharks."

"Coddle? What the hell are you talking about?" Jaxon felt hot around the collar. "I'm a success, Carlton. And we could have a fierce debate over whether it was because of you or in spite of you. But let's make one thing clear, I never looked to you to coddle me. I'll be damned if I'll make the same mistake my father did."

His grandfather turned beet-red. "Do not bring Junior into this. This is *not* about him."

Jaxon laughed. "Riiight. Let me tell you something. It has always been about him between me and you. You don't think I know that you look at me and see him? You don't think I know that you spent years trying to change the things in me that you hated about him?"

"Don't be ridiculous," he huffed, but his gaze darted around the room like a lost beacon.

"Admit it. *Please.* You never wanted me here. You took me in out of obligation, but you never *wanted* me."

"That's not true."

Jaxon waited for his grandfather's gaze, but clearly he was waiting in vain. "It is true. I could respect you more if you could just admit it." He glanced back down at the board and saw clearly the next move his grandfather was about to take. "Go ahead."

Carlton pretended like he didn't hear him.

"Do it."

"Forget it." He gave a careless wave toward the board as if the game suddenly didn't matter. "We can just play another time."

"What? *Now* you want to coddle me?"

Bullied into finishing the game, Carlton reached across the board and made his last move. "Checkmate."

Without another word, Jaxon grabbed his suit jacket and strolled out of his grandfather's office.

Richard Myers hadn't stopped thinking about Zora Campbell since the night he had met her, but a man's patience could only go so far. By now, he must've sent over a whole floral shop and still he hadn't heard a single word from her. However, he had no problems believing that Jaxon was also making his moves and probably getting much further with the curvy sexpot than Richard was at the moment. In fact, half of New York knew it if Page Six was to be believed. Eyewitness accounts, including one cab driver, leaked to the paper that Zora and Jaxon were seen in some sort of lovers' spat. And today the grapevine was buzzing about how Jaxon's engagement to adult entertainer Kitty Ervin was just a hoax. It figured. Something about that whole thing hadn't smelled right with him from the beginning.

Richard tossed the morning edition of the *New York Post* on a chair, but a few seconds later, his gaze snagged back on Zora's picture in the upper right-hand corner. It was actually something that he had been doing a lot lately. Not to the point that he was obsessed, but enough to know that he was in danger of falling head over heels.

He couldn't help it—especially since knowing that she was even more beautiful in person. And the idea that he could possibly lose out to Jaxon Landon *again* didn't sit too well. Somehow, someway, he needed to make sure that didn't happen.

Zora was surprised when *Vogue* came calling. Then she was pleased and flattered that they wanted to include her in a special edition cover—that included her and seven other supermodels from various decades. Of course more models meant more drama. To make sure that she kept her drama to a minimum, Zora made sure she was extra early to the photo shoot, kept her mouth shut and put a smile on her face.

Despite all of that, drama found her anyway.

"So what's this I hear about you and the so-called Prince of Wall Street?" the shoot's makeup artist asked before even introducing himself. "Are you guys really an item or what?"

Excuse you? "Now, you know better than that," she chided gently. "You really shouldn't believe everything you read in the papers."

"Chile, there's more truth in that trash than most people are willing to admit," he said, practically attacking her with a Kabuki powder brush. "'Course, a lot of us was just surprised to see *your* name printed in the gossip pages. Usually you keep your business out of the headlights. So y'all must have really caused a scene."

Zora kept her smile leveled at the appropriate

angle and didn't say another word until Keira Lee, famous from fashion's heroin-chic phase, plopped down in the chair beside her. In the fifteen years since she was at her peak, Keira looked as if she may have put on a whole whopping two pounds.

"Is there anything I can get you to drink, Ms. Lee?" an anxiety-riddled intern asked, rushing to her side.

"Water—and can you get me a couple of carrots from the buffet table? I'm famished."

"Right away," he said and then rushed off.

Keira's bored gaze finally landed on Zora. "Well, I'll be damned. If it isn't the world's number one Ebony Princess," she said in an exaggerated British accent.

Zora grimaced at the label Europeans had given her. "How are you, Keira?"

"High," she said matter-of-factly. "Either that or hungover."

"Still a party girl, I see."

"It passes the time. A chick gotta do something when she hits thirty and is considered over-the-hill in this industry." She accepted her bottled water and two carrots from the intern before her own makeup artist magically appeared at her side.

The comment was a bit of an exaggeration, but Zora understood what she meant. The modeling industry was fast, ruthless and short. Those that didn't educate themselves about their money and investments were just S.O.L. and usually ended up on reality rehab shows.

Keira had her own stint two years ago and clearly it hadn't worked.

As the morning went on and the other models showed up on set—most of them late as hell and costing the magazine a fortune, Zora began to relax. After all, she was in her element. She had never had a problem relating or, as some critics praised, making love to the camera.

"That's it, Zora," Erik Peterson, the magazine's photographer directed. "Beautiful! Beautiful!"

After completing one roll of film, she was sent back to wardrobe for a quick change, but the minute she made it over to the long racks of clothes, she was in for a surprise.

"Richard." She blinked and then looked around. "What are you doing here?"

His smile ballooned. "I'm here to see you." He offered up a single rose. "And to try one last time to ask you out."

Zora accepted the single rose and was just on the verge of declining his offer when she stopped herself. *What the hell?*

Chapter 12

Charity is big business in New York City. And tonight's annual gala for the Elton John AIDS Foundation brought out all the who's who. It wasn't the typical affair for a first date, but Zora was humbled and honored to attend on Richard's arm. And why not—the man hadn't done anything wrong. In fact, he had been nothing but a charming gentleman from the moment she'd met him.

She was the one who was tripping. All because Jaxon was a witness to the most embarrassing night of her life—well, the second most embarrassing night of her life. Plus, she wanted to put on a good face for the gossips at the *New York Post*. History proved that

hiding from scandal only gave rumormongers license
to escalate their outrageous charges. Hell, even Todd
kept calling, hoping to spin some great yarn about her
dating Wall Street royalty. To him and his kind there
was no such thing as bad publicity.

The fundraiser was being held at Cipriani's and
the event included the requisite red carpet and papa-
razzi. Richard, once again, was dressed to the nines
in an impeccably clean, black Armani suit. When
Zora had answered the door, she was struck by how
easily he could've made a living in the modeling
world himself—well, him *and* Jaxon.

Definitely Jaxon.

Stop it. Stop it. Don't go there. But hell, she'd
been telling herself that for the past week. All her
mental chastising seemed to do was make her think
about Jaxon even more—especially the way he stole
all the oxygen in a room, and the way she couldn't
think clearly whenever he was around *and* how
amazing his hand felt caressing the base of her clit
in the back of that restaurant.

Zora quivered from the memory.

"Are you cold?" Richard asked, as they inched
their way down the red carpet among flashing white
lights.

"No. No. I'm good." She reassured him with a
bright smile and then continued to pose for pictures
in a stunning red silk taffeta gown. Truth be told, she
was pleased that the dress was available on such

short notice, but her friendship with the designer pulled off a miracle.

"Who are you wearing, Ms. Campbell?" several reporters shouted at the same time.

"John Galliano," she responded and then gave everyone a back view.

More flashing lights and then, "Who are you with this evening?" one bold photograph asked.

Zora quickly returned to her date's side. "Richard Myers," she answered in her best bubbly voice.

"Is he your new boyfriend?" another shouted.

"Now. Now." She waved a finger at the press pool. "You guys know better than that."

"What about Jaxon Landon—the Prince of Wall Street? Are you two still together?"

Zora felt Richard's arm stiffen beneath hers. "Mr. Landon and I were never an item." She didn't know whether anyone bought it, but it was the answer she'd practiced in front of the mirror for two hours.

"What about the rumors that—"

Zora didn't get to hear the rest of the question because Richard directed her down the rest of the carpet like the damn thing suddenly caught fire. She didn't take it too personally. It couldn't be easy to stand there like a bump on a log while your date was being quizzed about some other man.

Walking into the building with its multicolumned exterior was like walking into a huge mausoleum with its opulent decor and sexy, dimly lit interior. Also upon entering, she and Richard were immediately enveloped by a throng of smiling and chatting people. Small talk was an art form among the rich. You smile a little, gush how fabulous everyone looks and then brag about some expensive piece of jewelry or exotic vacation you just took. You never *ever* talked about politics, books or money.

Money was implied.

"Looks like it's going to be a full house," Zora joked to Richard once they'd broken away from one laughing crowd.

However, Richard still looked peeved about what had happened on the red carpet and was slow to return the smile. Was he going to be like this for the rest of the night?

"Ah, Richard, you came." A boisterous older man with a mane of silvery hair and an outstretched hand greeted them.

"Mr. Colbert." Richard finally snapped out of his funk to shake hands with the man. "You know I make it here every year. I think what this foundation has managed to accomplish over the years is just extraordinary." Then he stopped as if remembering something. "You had a personal tragedy involving this cause, didn't you?"

Colbert nodded his head. "Yes, yes. Sadly, I lost my nephew to this awful disease. I have to tell you, it's very disappointing that with all our scientific advancements we haven't been able to find a cure."

"One day we will, sir. One day we will."

After a beat of silence, Colbert's sharp gray eyes darted in Zora's direction. "I see that your taste in women has improved." Laughing, he reached for her hand.

Richard turned toward her, his easy smile and charm fully restored. "Mr. Colbert, may I introduce you to the lovely Zora Campbell. Zora, Keith Colbert, the president of Epicon. My firm has been trying to convince this man to let us manage his portfolio for the past three years. He's as slippery as they come."

"What can I say, kid? There are a lot of offers on the table—most of them promising the world when all I want is the moon." He winked and then laughed at his own joke.

"It's nice to meet you," Zora said.

"The pleasure is all mine." Colbert bent over at the waist in a dramatic gesture and planted a kiss on the back of her hand. "I have to tell you that I'm a great admirer of your work."

"Thank you." Such gallantry won him another favorable smile from Zora.

"Colbert, old man!" someone shouted.

Zora turned in time to see another Armani-clad gentleman, waving frantically in the crowd.

"Ah, my grandson." Colbert laughed and gave a casual nod. "It was good, catching up with you,

Myers. We ought to do it again sometime." He started to walk off, but Richard held up an index finger to ask for another minute.

"Actually, my secretary called your office today to see if I could get on your schedule. I've finally worked out a package I think you might like."

Colbert huffed out his chest and shook his head. "I gotta be honest with you, Richard. I'm sort of leaning to signing up with Jaxon Landon."

Richard tensed again.

"What can I tell you, kid? The man has the Midas touch. Everyone wants to work with the Prince of Wall Street, right?" He laughed again and gave Richard a hearty pat on the shoulder. "I'm sure you understand. It's just business, kid."

Richard didn't answer. However, when Colbert tried to sidestep him, Richard blocked his exit. "I…think maybe there's something I need to be brought to your attention."

"Oh?" His smiling face turned somber. "Sounds serious."

Zora agreed but she didn't have any idea what was going on, but she could definitely tell Richard was angry. He had two protruding veins along his right temple that seemed ready to pop at any moment.

Richard started to say something else when his gaze snagged on someone across the room.

Zora and Colbert turned and tried to see who had grabbed his attention. Colbert may have been lost, but Zora's gaze had no trouble zeroing in on the towering Jaxon Landon. Instantly her body reacted. Parts of her grew warm, parts of her grew wet and the rest quivered with longing. Had he grown taller in the week since she'd last seen him— more buffed—and if possible, more handsome?

The vivid memory of his lips pressed against hers and his seductive scent enfolding her caused Zora's heart to race. Regret washed over her like a tsunami. There were at least a hundred ways she could've handled their last encounter better. Any of them would have been better than her running out of a crowded restaurant like she had a serial rapist on her heels.

"It *is* serious," Richard finally said. "You should talk to me before you finalize anything with Jaxon Landon."

Zora frowned and returned her attention back to Richard. She didn't like the tone of his voice. And there was something about the way he was staring at Jaxon that chilled Zora's blood.

"All right then," Colbert said soberly. "I'll make sure I get you worked into the schedule. Have your secretary call again."

Richard smiled, but it was a tight one that looked as if it hurt to produce. "Thank you, sir."

Free to leave, Colbert trickled back into the crowd, his recognizable laugh boomed from the next circle of friends.

"How about something to drink?" Richard asked

and then waved a waiter over. "I know I can definitely use one."

Seconds later, she was handed a flute of pink champagne and before she could bring the glass to her lips, Richard had drained his empty in one gulp. "Sooo. I take it that you and Jaxon don't exactly get along," she chanced saying.

Richard looked at her, hesitated. "Is that a question or a statement?"

"Maybe it's both."

He laughed. "It's complicated."

"Maybe you can simplify it for me?" she pressed.

He hesitated again. "I can't stand the smug sonofabitch," he said, leveling a hard stare. "For as long as I can remember, he's been a thorn in my side. First in school, when everyone thought he could do no wrong, to now when businessmen and colleagues call me *kid* and him the Prince of Wall Street."

"So you're…"

"What? Jealous?" he asked with a sinister smile. "Hardly. I'm competitive and determined. Just because I'm not among the flock that thinks the sun rises and sets on his ass doesn't mean I'm jealous. I just happen to see the devil through his sheep's clothing."

Zora blinked at him, mainly because she couldn't think of anything to say. His explanation didn't have any specifics and the hate radiating off him at the time wasn't like anything she'd ever witnessed before. True, she had her own haters—people targeting her because she was at one time at the top of the industry. She had always dismissed it as just being part of the game. But she had never seen hatred such as this up close and personal.

"Does my dislike for your rumored boyfriend make you uncomfortable?"

Zora gave a playful roll of her eyes. "C'mon. You know better than that. He's not my boyfriend."

Richard just studied her.

"What?" she asked defensively.

He shook his head. "Nothing. I'm just trying to figure out whether you're lying."

Richard's blunt statement stunned her.

"C'mon. Don't look at me like that. Surely, you can understand my position. The night we met you claimed that you didn't know him or the Landons but you have the funny habit of popping up in some unconventional scenarios with him."

Now she was angry. "If I recall, you were the one that led me out onto that balcony."

"And the restaurant?"

So that's what this is all about! "I was on a date—with someone else. Jaxon sort of came to my rescue. That's all."

"Ahh." Richard bobbed his head as he swiveled back in Jaxon's direction. "The hero routine. Figures."

Zora didn't like the direction of the conversation and hated that she'd even pursued this line of questioning.

"Still," Richard said, swinging his attention back toward her. "I don't think that I'm too far off in saying that there's definitely something between you two whether you realize it or not."

"Don't be ridiculous," she said flippantly and waved a waiter over for another glass of champagne. Now she was the one in desperate need of a drink.

"Like right now. I've never seen him work so hard trying to ignore someone."

"Maybe he doesn't like *you,* either."

Unfazed, Richard kept his eyes leveled on her. "I was referring to you."

"Pleeeaase."

Richard laughed. "Methinks thou doth protest too much."

"And methinks thou is paranoid," she volleyed back with annoyance. Instead of shutting him up, the charming bastard just laughed harder.

"Okay. You win. You say that nothing is going on, then I believe you."

Clearly now in a good mood, his arm snaked around her waist. She tried hard not to tense up, but she wasn't too successful.

"Just trust that I know Jaxon better than you. He's a man you wouldn't want to tangle with. He will use anyone and anything to get what he wants. Take this farce of an engagement. He's not fooling anyone so why is he doing it? And his supposed winning streak? I've never heard of anyone being able to post the sort of profits he's been touting since Bernie Madoff."

Richard's paranoia proved to be contagious. Jaxon's simple explanation for the fake engagement did sound sort of fishy. And did he try to use her unfortunate position at the restaurant last week to his advantage? He knew that she was good for the money, but he'd threatened to call the cops unless she agreed to go out with him. What kind of man would do such a thing?

A new group found their way over to the couple and Zora found herself swept up in another round of small talk. Midway through the pleasantries, Zora was fully aware when Jaxon noticed her in the room. The weight of his gaze was so heavy her knees were seconds from buckling beneath her. Yet, whenever she looked in his direction, he appeared to be engrossed in his own conversations.

The one gaze she did manage to find at every turn was his *fake* fiancée's, Kitty. Despite the rather compromising position Zora had last seen the woman, Zora attempted to smile, but the frosty stare she received and the way Kitty kept clinging onto Jaxon spoke volumes. The couple may not have been engaged, but the two were clearly lovers.

Jealousy kicked Zora hard in the gut as she quickly pulled her gaze away.

Bells jingled around the crowd as the waitstaff started opening doors for the auditorium.

"I guess that means the concert is about ready to get underway," Richard said, offering Zora his arm.

She smiled and looped her arm through his, but as they walked toward the doors, the weight of Jaxon's gaze returned.

Chapter 13

Jaxon was pissed.

No. He was beyond pissed and didn't know what to do about it. Sure, he could've strolled over to Richard and punched him dead in his smug face, but that would only make him feel good for a couple of seconds—max. The evitable fallout and arrest for turning this exclusive and elaborate fundraiser into a Las Vegas boxing match would undoubtedly reward him with another week in those ridiculous gossip rags.

Still, his hands kept clenching and unclenching at his sides.

Maybe it would've helped if he'd at least had

some sort of heads-up that Zora would be attending the night's function, he would've been better prepared. As it was, he was completely caught off guard and the added punch to the gut was to see her with that *dickhead*.

"Are you all right?" Kitty must've asked him a hundred times tonight.

Each time, he would assure his date that he was fine, but nothing was further from the truth. He and Kitty were friends, but he wasn't crazy enough to talk to her about another woman. He did have a little more sense than that. However, he did tell her that after tonight her services were no longer needed. The charade had gone on for too long as it was and Kitty had been compensated enough to help with her grandmother's medical bills.

For the past week, he'd been beating himself up over how things had gone so wrong at the restaurant. He wasn't surprised that Zora had backed out of their deal, but he was bothered that she had resurrected a wall between them. He'd been shocked and amused to see the incident in the papers, but then realized that it was probably the price of dealing with a celebrity.

A part of him said just let it go. Clearly, she didn't want anything to do with him and he certainly wasn't used to chasing a woman who wouldn't give him the time of day. But the other part of him, the stronger part, couldn't let it go. Couldn't let her go.

* * *

Zora should've been having a good time.

Richard had returned to being charming and the awards ceremony was educational and heartwarming and the musical entertainment was outstanding. However, Zora couldn't allow herself to completely enjoy the spectacular fundraising. The hardest part was pretending that she was having a good time.

She never claimed to be a great actress. Every time Richard would glance her way she was sure that he saw right through her. If he did, then he was a better actor because he never let on.

"I'll be right back," she announced suddenly.

Richard quirked an inquisitive eyebrow.

"Need to go to the ladies' room."

Richard stepped into the aisle and allowed her out of their row of seats.

"I'll be right back," she promised, smiling.

"I'll be here." He winked.

Zora easily made her way out of the auditorium, but finding the nearest ladies' room felt more like a treasure hunt. Finally in the midst of this massive labyrinth, she found the powder room. *If it had been a snake it would have bitten me,* she joked to herself.

Just as she was about to push the door open, she felt it. Turning, she swung her gaze wide around the imposing building. Like all the times before, her inner homing device had no trouble locating Jaxon. He was talking to a gentleman in low tones and seeming to ignore her. That bothered her. Sure, she was the one to run out in damn hysterics in front of him, and true, she did renege on the deal struck in the restaurant, but for some reason she felt slighted that *he* was the one mad at her.

Okay. It's official. I've lost my mind. But even knowing that she was thinking illogically didn't change the way she felt. Maybe she did owe the man an explanation—but the only thing that she could say in her defense was that she'd overreacted.

Jaxon and his friend shook hands and the other man started to stride in the opposite direction. Jaxon's gaze passed over her like she was just a piece of furniture and then he proceeded to move back toward the auditorium.

Hurt, Zora knew that if she was going to apologize, she needed to do it now.

"Jaxon," she called, but her voice sounded as though it had suddenly been seized by that damn bullfrog again. Still, Zora was sure that he'd heard her, but he kept moving.

"Jaxon, wait!" She gathered the side of her gown and ran toward him. Her shout caught the ear of a few partiers, milling outside the auditorium, but there were no more than a handful at best. At the moment the only thing that mattered was that Jaxon's long strides slowed down.

When she finally reached his side, she was out of breath and relieved that she hadn't broken her neck running in Manolo Blahniks.

"I need to talk to you," she said.

Jaxon stopped, drew a deep breath and turned toward her.

Faced with clear hostility, Zora lost her voice for a few seconds. Jaxon had always been an imposing figure, dangerous to her peace of mind, but now she sensed another type of danger.

"What is it?" he asked. His voice was low and flat.

"I—I just want to, um—" She tried to swallow that annoying frog in her throat, but the damn thing felt wedged in there pretty tight.

Jaxon's jaw tightened.

"Look. I'm sorry, all right?" she finally spit out. "That night at the restaurant—I *may* have overreacted." There. She said it. In the ensuing silence each second felt like an hour and somehow Zora found the courage to look him in the eye—but she didn't keep the connection long. Her emotions were all over the place, but that was quickly becoming the norm whenever she was around him.

"Is that all?" he asked.

Zora panicked. It was clear that he was just seconds away from dismissing her and she couldn't think of a damn thing to say to stop him. "Yeah," she said, now reduced to a whisper. "I guess that's it."

Jaxon nodded. "Then I'm glad that you got that off your chest." He turned and breezed through the doors of the auditorium.

Zora just stood there. Her mind was whirling as embarrassment crept up her neck and face. "Okay. I guess that's that." Her eyes burned with brimming tears, but she fought them back and marched her way toward the bathroom. What else could she do?

Entering the posh and elegantly decorated room, she was instantly met with a heady mix of expensive perfume and a citrus blend of some type of air freshener. The elaborate bathroom looked like a cross between a museum and a day spa—complete with chaise lounges, toiletries and flowers.

The sudden quiet allowed Zora a brief moment for her to take a deep breath and relax. To her great relief there were only a couple of women putting a few polishing touches on their makeup in the mirror. By the time Zora approached, they had turned away and were now heading their way to the exit. As they passed they nodded in a silent greeting and kept moving.

Alone, Zora took a moment to make sure that everything was tucked and lying the way it should be. Her long hair was still pinned up tight and looked just as fresh as it did when she'd left her penthouse apartment. The only thing she saw was that her lipstick could use a little touch-up. Not in any great hurry to return to the concert, she opened her clutch bag and removed her Guerlain lipstick.

She didn't want to think about what had just transpired between her and Jaxon. He was clearly upset and she'd simply either waited too long to apologize or…hell, what does it matter?

Zora sniffed, feeling those damn tears again. What was with her? She hardly knew the man.

She heard the bathroom door open, but didn't pay any attention to who'd walked inside. Zora was too busy refreshing her lipstick and making kissy faces at the mirror to make sure that she had full coverage, when came that familiar feeling.

She froze. In the next second she shifted her gaze in the mirror and then sucked in a startled breath.

Jaxon smiled and then moved over to the stalls and started checking to see if they were alone.

"What are you doing in here?"

"Clearly, I came to speak with you," he said in a bored voice.

Zora spun around. "You can't come in here. What if someone catches you?"

His eyes finally softened as he gave her an amused grin. "What? You didn't enjoy our time in the tabloids?"

"Not particularly."

"Then I guess I better lock the door." He strolled back across the bathroom and did just that.

Speechless, Zora watched him. She would be

lying to herself if she said that she wasn't happy to see him, especially after that fiasco of an apology she'd just performed minutes ago.

The door locked, Jaxon moved to the center of the room and folded his arms as he looked around. "It's pretty nice in here. I'd always heard rumors that the ladies' rooms were much nicer. Are they all like this?"

It was a strange question. "Generally, they're pretty nice." She shrugged at the awkward small talk, but then those long hourly seconds returned while he considered her. "You know, I find your taste in men rather interesting. Do you have a special knack for attracting losers or are you just in a slump?"

"You tell me."

Jaxon shook his head. "He's all wrong for you."

Zora's brows stretched high. "Don't tell me you came in here to give me dating tips."

"Maybe you can use them."

"This coming from a man with a stripper for a fake fiancée?"

He smiled. "Touché."

Zora lifted her chin in silent victory and then capped her tube of lipstick and plopped it back into her clutch purse.

"So what are we doing?" he asked.

She cocked her head as if she didn't understand his question.

"Are we playing games or are we going to do this?"

That damn frog was back.

Jaxon moved toward her. "Because I gotta tell you, I don't usually put up with even half the drama that's been whirling around us since we met. But there's just something about you…"

Zora tried to back up but then found herself pressed up against the vanity sink. Once she chanced a look into his handsome face, she found that she couldn't break away. His black eyes devoured yet caressed her at the same time. His familiar seductive scent weakened her knees and damn near turned her spine into Jell-O. She couldn't fight the hypnotic trance stealing across her.

"For some reason I can't get you out of my head." His lips quirked up in a half smile. "You're in my thoughts—my dreams." He shook his head. "You're beautiful. But you're trouble."

Zora's heart raced. "I—I…" *Damn. Why can't I talk?*

"Why did you run that night?" he asked bluntly. "Truthfully."

She swallowed and then tried to talk, but it was simply impossible. She needed him to back up for a minute so she could think. But then she made the mistake in reaching out and pressing a hand against his hard chest. The sudden shock of electricity didn't just burn her, it scorched.

She jumped and then tried to remove her hand, but lightning fast Jaxon grabbed her hand and held it in place.

"You feel it, too, don't you?"

Lie. Lie. Lie. But what was the point in lying? Was she supposed to stand there and prove how strong she was? Did the idea of being in control mean that much?

"I don't want to play games," he said. "I want you."

Zora tried swallowing again.

Someone pushed against the bathroom door. "Hey, why is this thing locked?" a woman asked in the hallway.

"I don't know. Let's just go use the other one," another woman answered.

In the bathroom's silence, Zora and Jaxon stared into each other's eyes.

"I better get back to my date," she whispered.

"In a minute." Jaxon removed her clutch from her other hand and tossed it onto the counter behind her. "We're going to finish this conversation."

Zora's heart was beating so loud that she just barely made out what he said.

"I'm trying to figure out what I'm going to do about you. And we're not leaving until we come to some kind of understanding."

"Jaxon, I—I only wanted to apologize b-because I realized that I'd overreacted. I—I thought that we could just put it behind us and maybe we could be friends."

"I'm not interested in being your friend," he said bluntly. "I want more…and I *know* you do, too. So let's put the bullshit aside and get a couple things straight."

Zora's eyes widened.

"Now I don't know what kind of men you're used to, but I'm not down for a bunch of head games and drama. You made a deal with me and you broke it."

"That deal was coerced. You were trying to take advantage of the situation."

"Of course I did."

She blinked stupidly at him.

"What? You think I'm *not* going to use every opportunity to my advantage? What, you think I'm another one of those weak brothers who is just going to pass you a business card and hope one day you'd call?"

His assessment struck the bull's-eye.

"Your problem is men let you get away with too much bullshit. You're used to being in control and that shit isn't going to fly with me."

There was no question that he meant what he said. Zora's fierce independence wanted to protest, but the rest of her was completely turned on by Jaxon's dominance.

"The point is," he continued, "I *want* you." He

cupped her chin with his fingers. "You need to decide—right here, right now—whether you want me, too."

Zora opened her mouth, but before she could answer, he pressed a finger against her ruby red lips.

"Before you answer, you need to know that there's no half stepping with this. If we're going to do this, then we're gonna do this right." He removed his finger. "So what's it going to be?"

Light-headed and completely turned on, Zora gave the only answer she could: the truth. "I want you, too."

Chapter 14

It wasn't the right time or place, but the moment Zora made her confession, Jaxon couldn't refrain from devouring her beautiful full lips in a hungry kiss. Once he got started, he couldn't get enough. She was sweet, toxic and addictive all at the same time. When she slid her silky tongue into his mouth, his mind reeled into another world. Nothing else mattered. He had to have her.

All of her.

With little effort, he picked up the five-foot-ten model, set her on the vanity counter and then proceeded to pull her silk gown up her long legs. Still he couldn't get enough of her delicate lips. So soft. So moist. So sweet.

After her lips, he feasted on her tongue while simultaneously working his hands up the inside of her gown and then seizing control of her lace panties. Her mouth and his anticipation were giving him a fever. Either that or the huge marble bathroom had suddenly turned into a furnace. As far as he was concerned the damn place could've been on fire and he wasn't about to go anywhere. Getting inside her was more important than life.

For Zora, the need to feel Jaxon inside her blocked all reason and common sense. His kisses tasted like the richest chocolate and his touch felt like the softest silk. Needless to say her body was already quivering with miniorgasms and by the time he'd pulled her panties from her hips, she knew that they were dewy wet.

"Lean back," he said. His voice was as paper-thin as hers. "I want to taste you."

It took everything she had to pull away from his luscious mouth, but she did as she was told and leaned back until her head and shoulders pressed against the bathroom mirror.

"Why the hell is this door locked?" Someone attempted to come in. They pushed a few times and even knocked.

But nothing. Absolutely nothing was going to disturb this groove.

Zora watched as Jaxon hiked her legs until the back of her high-heeled shoes sat up on the edge of the counter and her legs made the perfect V before him.

Clearly Jaxon was a man who was used to taking his time. He didn't just plunge in to get to the nitty-gritty, but instead planted wonderful small kisses from her knee and all the way down her inner thigh. She was a whimpering mess by the time he reached her wet pussy. When his mouth came down to kiss her lower lip, she shamelessly lifted her hips to try to meet his mouth sooner.

Jaxon smiled, and then rewarded her greediness by sliding his long tongue under the base of her clit.

"Aaaah," she gasped while her belly and thighs quivered with aftershocks.

He'd always known that she would be sweet, but he certainly didn't expect her to taste like peaches. It was so good to him that he stretched his tongue in deeper and then rotated it around to sap up as much juice as he possibly could.

"Ooooh." Zora sighed and then reached up to squeeze her own breasts. At the next long flick of Jaxon's tongue, she hissed and squirmed like a snake.

"Damn, baby. This is some good pussy," he panted before plunging in again. He licked and sucked on her clit like a lollipop.

Zora couldn't stop moaning and the acoustics in the bathroom made it sound like she was giving a concert of her own.

"Hey, I think somebody is in there!" There was another knock on the door.

They could knock until the cows came home, Zora wasn't about to move. Not with the feeling of a 6.0 earthquake rumbling inside her body. It was like nothing she'd ever felt before. She wasn't afraid of it. In fact, her hips were pumping as hard as Jaxon's tongue now slapped against her inner walls.

When it was seconds from detonation, Zora reached down between her legs and grabbed hold of Jaxon's head and locked him into position. Her sighs raced up the musical scale until she practically hit a high C and a white blinding light flashed behind her closed eyes. To her surprise, it wasn't just one big explosion, but this long winding wave that seemed to go forever.

"C'mere, baby," Jaxon said, standing.

Lazily, Zora pulled herself up and was greeted with a soul-stirring kiss where she could taste her own juices off his lips. It was a different experience for her. Naughty. Dirty. Erotic.

"Unzip me," he ordered.

Zora obeyed though her fingers were moving too slow for her own liking. Once she had him unzipped and his pants unbuttoned, a big smile framed the corners of her lips at the magnificent sight of his big, thick cock. It was just as beautiful as the last time she'd seen it—and just as mouth-watering.

"Go ahead. Touch it."

She didn't need any further encouragement. Zora wrapped her small hand around the smooth pole and watched as it stretched up another good inch.

"I think it likes you," Jaxon joked, leaning in for another kiss.

Zora moaned but continued to stroke him like she'd just been given a new toy to play with.

"You know what I want to do to you, right?" he panted.

She nodded.

"Tell me."

Boldly, she met his lustful stare. "You want to fuck me."

"You're damn right, baby." He kissed her. "Any objections?"

Zora shook her head.

"Are you sure?" he asked. "I don't want you running out of here if you're not sure."

Zora couldn't think of any other place she would rather be than sitting on that counter with Jaxon standing between her legs. "I'm sure."

Jaxon kissed her again. "Good answer."

A condom was produced from his back pocket and Zora did the honor of stretching the latex over the thick mushroom head of his cock and then sliding it down the long shaft.

"Get up and turn around."

Zora quickly scrambled off the counter and then turned and faced herself in the mirror. She was immediately struck by how good they looked together and then shortly after, how good he looked—period.

"Bend over, baby." He gave her a gentle push against her back and then hiked her gown up over her hips. "Spread your legs."

She took the order without question and then grabbed hold of the faucet when she felt the head of his dick slide in from the back.

"Ssssss," they both hissed as he eased inside.

Zora leaned up on her toes, but Jaxon gently pressed her back down. Even though she was struggling to take him all in, she was completely turned on by watching the emotions rippling across his handsome face. Inch by glorious inch, he tightened his jaw while still sucking in air through his clenched teeth.

Zora's knees buckled, but the pleasure hurt so good.

"Look at me," he said.

She found his serious gaze in the mirror and then watched him as his hips delivered the first slow, deep strokes. "Oooh," she moaned with tears filling her eyes. Nothing on earth should *ever* feel like this.

"You like that, baby?"

"Oh, God, yes."

He reached up and cupped her breasts into his large hands. As he squeezed and pinched, he stroked deeper and deeper. "Keep looking at me, baby. I want to watch you come."

Zora tried her best to maintain eye contact but her

neck kept rolling back and her eyes wanted to close. This was ecstasy—pure and simple.

"Somebody is having sex in there!"

"Aah. Aah." Zora wanted to shut up but she couldn't.

At first Jaxon was rocking her deep and slow, but when his body continued to heat up, he started pumping at a feverish pace. He had never had anyone like her before. There was something about the way her silky inner walls flexed and relaxed that had him thinking he was falling in love.

Love? What the hell was wrong with him? He hardly knew her. But yet, somehow that didn't matter. There was something strong at play here. The normal rules were now thrown out the window. He had known lust for most of his life and what he was feeling right now didn't belong in that category. This was something bigger and stronger than he was.

The playa in him wanted to hit this and run—but the *man* in him wasn't going to allow it.

Zora came once.

Twice.

And on the third time, she felt tiny electric currents rippling throughout her entire body. Jaxon's breathing started to strain and the grip on her hips tightened.

"Oh, damn, Z. Sssss. Oh, damn."

"You're coming, baby?" she asked, throwing her ass back at him and stealing a little control for herself. "Hmm?" She threw it a little harder while her own juices started to rush down her thighs. He was reaching his peak and she knew it. She watched his face as it twisted and untwisted.

"Fuck! I'm going to come," he announced.

"Yeah?" Her ass rocked harder. "Look at me."

His gaze shot toward hers in the mirror and the next second he was shouting her name. Coming, too, Zora grabbed hold of two sink faucets and coated his cock with her sweet juices.

Jaxon collapsed against her, panting and kissing a fine sheen of sweat. "There's no going back," he said. "You're mine now."

After a wild and impulsive quickie in the bathroom, it was rather easy for Zora to put herself together again. It was getting out of that bathroom that was a little more difficult. After hearing at least a dozen different women try to come in, she feared that once they opened the door, there would be a crowd of curious females along with a few cameras snapping in her face.

Not to mention, she wouldn't know what to do if her indiscretion reached her date. Given Richard's visceral hatred toward Jaxon it could make the night a little awkward. Hell, she had a hard time believing the sudden turn of events herself.

"I'll keep these," Jaxon said, tucking her red lace panties into his inside jacket pocket.

Zora arched an amused brow.

"A memento," he answered the unasked question. "Plus it will give me a thrill knowing that you're prancing around this fancy place with no drawers on." He winked.

"No fair."

"All is fair in love."

Zora's heart kicked. However, she didn't question the statement. Most likely, he meant it as a joke anyway. It was waaay too soon for either of them to be talking about the *L* word.

"Are you ready?" he asked. His suit was back to looking picture-perfect and he was handing over her clutch purse.

"I guess as ready as I'll ever be." Zora gave him a weak smile and in return he gave her a kiss that made her feel like she didn't care what awaited her outside the door. But she was more than surprised to see who was outside the bathroom.

"Melanie," Zora stuttered and then glanced around the hall.

"Uh-huh." Melanie folded her arms.

Veronica and Jessica were having a hard time trying not to laugh.

Zora was sure that she was every shade of red in the Crayola box. "I, uh, we were, um…"

"Save it." Melanie walked up to her and took her by the elbow. "Can I speak with you for a moment?" She directed Zora away from Jaxon before either of them had a chance to object. "What in the hell do you think you're doing?" she hissed. "You don't put out on the first date!"

"We're not here together," Zora whispered back.

"Which makes it even worse," Melanie said and stomped her gorgeous pumps against the marble floor.

"I—didn't, i-it just happened," Zora sputtered.

"Sex in a public bathroom doesn't just happen," Melanie continued, pulling Zora away.

"Where are you taking me?"

"Back to your *date*."

Chapter 15

When Zora reached the door of the auditorium, she nearly crashed head-on with her date.

"Ah, there you are." Richard chuckled. "I was just about to go and launch a search party for you." He glanced from her to Melanie and her two nieces. "Is everything all right?"

"Um. Yeah. Everything's great," Melanie croaked.

Melanie jumped in with a quick lie. "Yes, uh, just got caught up chitchatting."

Veronica and Jessica looked away. Clearly they didn't want to have anything to do with this monstrous lie.

Zora fluttered on a butterfly smile, but felt uneasy about this whole thing.

"Well, I guess we'll catch up with you later," Melanie said to Zora and added a sharp narrowed look that told her to get back on her best behavior. "C'mon, girls."

Completely chastised, Zora glanced at her date. "Is the concert almost over?"

Richard's forehead wrinkled as if he sensed that something was wrong. "No, but they should be wrapping it up soon." He stared at her for a moment but then gently wrapped an arm around her waist. "Do you want to go back inside or…" He stiffened.

Zora followed his gaze. Of course, it had landed on Jaxon as he strolled out from the very hallway that she and her small entourage had just left.

Richard's hard stare sliced toward her. A question reflected in his eyes.

Zora played it cool and offered him the weakest of smiles. "We better get back in there. I don't want to miss the grand finale." She pulled Richard along as if that would somehow erase the suspicion brewing in his head.

Once in their seats, she went through great lengths to make sure to keep her attention focused on the center stage. She prayed that her performance was spot-on, but doubt crept up along her spine as she now felt the weight of two heavy stares.

The one from Jaxon in the back of the auditorium and the one from the man standing next to her.

The rest of the concert passed by in one long endless blur. Zora mingled and made small talk until her brain felt numb. Just when her favorite shoes started cutting off the circulation in her feet, Richard finally asked whether she was ready to go.

Oh, Lord, yes! "Sure. If you're ready."

Richard nodded and expertly withdrew her from the crowd. Zora would have loved to believe that it was just her imagination that Richard had become unusually silent and distant since she'd returned to the concert, just as she would have loved to believe that she imagined a few attendees were gossiping about a couple having sex in one of the ladies' bathrooms. She heard them, but she prayed that Richard didn't.

The moment the driver slammed the door to the limousine, Zora felt as if she'd just been locked inside a tomb. Neither she nor Richard said anything the first fifteen minutes into the drive. The tension between them was tight and fear trickled from nowhere. When she finally chanced a look in his direction, she was taken aback at his hardened face.

"Is there something wrong?" she asked and then held her breath.

Richard arched a well-groomed brow. "What could possibly be wrong? I went out with a beautiful and intelligent woman tonight. I mingled with friends and colleagues. There was good food—great music." He shrugged his shoulders. "All in all, I have to say I had a wonderful night."

Zora swallowed. She had an eerie feeling that she was in the middle of a dangerous cat and mouse game.

"How about you?" he asked. "Did you *enjoy* your evening?"

She swallowed again. "I had a wonderful time."

"Good." He cheered up. "Maybe we can do it again sometime?"

She smiled, hesitated. "Sure. That—that sounds nice."

Richard turned and looked out the limousine's dark windows.

Half an hour later, they arrived at her penthouse apartment building. Zora tried her best to talk Richard out of walking her to her door. But it didn't work.

"Now what kind of gentleman would I be if I didn't at least walk you to your door?"

Zora smiled and relented under his steadfast determination. After all, there was nothing unusual about his request—in fact, it was customary for a man to walk his date to her door.

"Good evening, Ms. Campbell," Billy, the stoic doorman, greeted with the slightest tip of his head and then pulled opened the door.

"Evening, Billy."

Richard slid an arm around Zora and ignored the doorman.

Zora frowned at his rudeness and wished that she could just race across the lobby to hurry up this whole affair. The sooner she ended this night, the better as far as she was concerned.

However, Richard seemed content with a leisurely stroll. "This is a very nice building—great location," he commented. "How long have you lived here?"

"Not long. Three years." Zora shrugged, punched the elevator button and then began nervously tapping her foot while she waited.

"Don't tell me you're anxious to get rid of me already?"

"What? Huh?"

Richard glanced down at her foot.

She quickly stopped tapping. "Oh, no. I, um—" She searched for a lie. "I just really have to go to the bathroom."

Richard's brows stretched.

"Um, the old bladder isn't what it used to be," she joked.

He didn't laugh.

A bell dinged and the elevator doors slid open. Together, Zora and Richard stepped inside the large steel box. She went from one tomb to another. Standing inside the elevator, Zora unleashed a wild scream inside her head. Just a few more minutes and this date would soon be history.

In the back of her mind, she knew that she was

wrong for her behavior tonight. Who the hell screws one man while they're on a date with another? She had never in her life behaved in such a manner, but she would be lying if she said that she was sorry for it.

The elevator bell dinged again. Zora smiled and led Richard out of the elevator and marched over to her front door.

"Well," she said with a big dramatic sigh. "I guess this is it."

Richard just gave her an amused chuckle. "You're not going to invite me in for a nightcap?"

The smile on Zora's face dimmed. "I, um."

"C'mon. One drink," he said. "It's not like we really had any one-on-one time tonight."

"I don't know," Zora said, shaking her head. "It's getting pretty late and—"

"Aww. C'mon. One drink," Richard pressed.

Zora blinked.

"Would it help if I promised to be on my best behavior?"

She smiled but still hesitated. "It's just that I have a very early-morning appointment."

"Ten minutes," he wrangled. "Ten minutes and I'll be out of your hair."

Zora studied him. She definitely wanted to end the night, but she also felt guilty about her behavior. "All right," she said. "One drink."

Richard's sly smile returned. "Great."

Zora slid her key into the lock and invited Richard inside.

"Beautiful," Richard complimented when she flipped on the lights to her four thousand square foot penthouse. It was picture-perfect, like a designer magazine spread with sleek hardwood floors and panoramic views in every direction.

"Thank you," Zora said. "What would you like to drink?" she asked, walking up to her large oak and stained-glass bar. She plopped down her clutch purse on the counter and immediately started reaching for glasses.

"Oh, I don't know. How about a Scotch and soda?"

"One Scotch and soda coming up."

"None for you?" He followed her over to the bar.

"I told you. It's kind of late."

Richard waved a finger at her. "It's not polite to let a man drink alone." He smiled, but it didn't quite reach his eyes.

"Maybe I'll have a small one," she said.

"Good girl." He winked.

Zora quickly made their drinks, walked around the bar and handed him his glass. "Here you go, Mr. Myers."

Richard smiled as he accepted the glass. "You know there was something I've been meaning to ask you tonight," he said.

"Oh? What's that?" She pressed her own glass to her lips.

"Well, I was curious to know just how big a *fool* you thought I was?"

Zora sputtered and choked on her drink. When she finally cleared her windpipe, she glanced up at Richard. "What?"

"Pleeease." Richard's face turned as hard and expressionless as stone. "You're not that good of an actress."

She blinked stupidly at him.

"So what is it?" he asked. "You and Jaxon are in on this together?" His eyes narrowed. "Are you his little *spy* or something?"

Zora had no idea what the hell he was talking about and she had *no* desire to find out. She turned and set her drink down on the bar. "I think it's time you left."

"I'm not ready to leave." He threw his glass across the room and then snatched her up by her wrist.

"Oww. Let go of me!"

Richard's hold grew more painful as he crushed her body against his. "What? You think I don't know what the fuck happened tonight? You think I didn't notice that you and Jaxon disappeared at the same time? The same *damn* time that people were whispering about a couple fucking in the goddamn bathroom?"

Before Zora could say anything, Richard's hand shot out and whipped across her face. Zora's head snapped back.

Richard's grip shifted to her shoulders where he then proceeded to shake the hell of her. "Let me tell you something. I'm nobody's fool." He shook her harder. "Do you hear me?"

His hand whipped across her face again and she screamed, *"Fire!"*

"Shut the fuck up!" He slapped her again and then proceeded to drag her across the room to her white leather couch.

She kicked and screamed the entire way. *"Fire!"*

Slap.

"Get out! Get out!"

"Oh, no." He struggled to hold her down while he fumbled with his zipper. "I'm not leaving here until I get a little bit of what you gave Jaxon tonight."

"No!"

"What? I'm not good enough for you? You can only be his ho, is that it?"

"Get off! Get off!" She swung her legs, her arms—anything that could move, trying to get him off, but he seemed to have the strength of an army.

When she screamed again, he covered her face with a pillow.

Chapter 16

Jaxon debated whether to go home or to make a surprise visit at Zora's place. It wasn't like him to want to do a roll by. But after that short passionate session at the fundraiser tonight, Jaxon's body craved more. It hadn't been easy watching Zora parade around on Richard's arm. Somehow he survived the torture, but that might not hold up if he didn't see her again tonight.

"It's our last night out together, isn't it?" Kitty asked.

Troubled by her sad tone, Jaxon looked at her and upon reading her broken heart, he nodded. "Kitty, I—I thought that—"

Her ruby-colored lips hitched up into a half

smile. "Hey, you can't blame a girl for hoping." She glanced away.

Jaxon struggled to find the right words. In his mind this had always been a business arrangement. Certainly they had been intimate in the past, but not in these recent weeks when she posed as his fiancée. "I'm sorry if you feel like perhaps I led you on in any way."

"No. No. Don't be sorry." Her eyes found his again.

"Katherine, you are an extraordinary woman. One day you're going to make some lucky son of a bitch a *very* happy man."

"But it's never going to be you," she butted in.

Jaxon's face softened with sympathy. "I'm sorry."

Kitty nodded, but remained in her seat for a few long seconds while she fought back tears.

"Kitty—"

"Stop," she whispered. "It's not you or anything you've done. In fact, you've been wonderful. If it had not been for this generous offer, there would have been no way I could've taken care of my grandmother's medical bills. I'm the one that let myself get caught up in some…silly fantasy. The Prince of Wall Street and the Queen of Burlesque. Quite a headline, huh?" She swiped a finger beneath her eye and caught a lone tear.

Guilt still settled across Jaxon's shoulders.

"Do you love her?" she asked suddenly.

Jaxon should've questioned who she was referring to, but he knew because he was wondering the same thing. "I just met her," he said.

"That's not what I asked."

"I…" He quickly mulled the question over again. "I have very strong feelings for her." He stopped, but then had to continue. "Feelings I never felt for another woman before."

Kitty flinched.

"I'm sorry," he added, realizing that he'd shoved his foot into his mouth.

"No need. You're just being honest and…I appreciate that," she said. "You've always been honest with me." She leaned over in her seat and pressed a kiss against his cheek. "Don't worry. You're still my favorite customer." A ghost of a smile returned to her lips. "See you at the club?"

He smiled, not wanting to commit to anything.

"Good night," she said.

Jaxon reached for his door.

"No. That's not necessary. I can walk myself up. Good night," she said again, and then climbed out of the limousine.

Jaxon remained seated and watched as his date walked into her apartment building. Katherine Ervin was certainly one fine act.

Seconds later, Kwan jumped back behind the driver's wheel and the glass partition that separated them slid down. "Where to, boss?" His young, eager eyes met Jaxon's in the rearview mirror.

Jaxon thought it over, reached into his jacket and pulled out the red panties. "Head back on up to Time Warner Centre."

Kwan's face twisted in confusion.

Jaxon rolled his eyes. "Go out of here and take a right at the next light."

"You got it, boss." Kwan pulled away from the curb and, by the usual blare of a horn, cut off another driver.

Jaxon just rolled his eyes and shook his head.

Zora fought for breath as her clothes were being ripped from her body. From behind the pillow, her arms flailed out and hit her target upside his head a few times—hard. Yet, his assault continued. She screamed loud and hard, but most of the sound was being absorbed by the pillow.

She kicked and bucked, but Richard's weight was cradled across her waist and she couldn't get him off or do much damage.

"Stop it. Stop it," he hissed down at her. "What the hell are you screaming for? Isn't this the way you whores like it?"

Whap! She landed another smack across his face.

Richard added more pressure onto the pillow and Zora felt her lungs begin to struggle.

He growled. "You were fucking him, weren't you?" He removed the pillow from her face. "Admit it!"

In the second that it took for her to suck in some oxygen, he delivered another blow across her face to knock it all out.

"Tell me the truth." His hand locked around her neck. "Tell me the truth!" He took his other hand and tried to jam it in between her legs but she locked her thighs as tight as she could.

Oh, God. Don't let this happen. Please, don't let this happen. Hot tears brimmed and then fell from the corners of her eyes like a waterfall. This simply couldn't be happening to her.

Zora redoubled her efforts by turning her long nails into claws and raking them down the side of his face.

Richard yelped and loosened his hold.

Zora came up and jabbed two fingers directly into his eyes.

He howled, crumbled back and then launched toward her, blindly.

Then—a miracle.

"Get the fuck off her!" a voice thundered from above.

Richard's weight was lifted off her body.

The sudden available oxygen seemed to escalate her dizziness. There was a loud crash and Zora managed to pull herself up to see Jaxon, her towering savior, deliver a hard right hook across Richard's jaw.

Richard's head snapped back so hard, it was a wonder how the damn thing was still attached.

"What, you like beating on women?" *Bam!*

Zora flinched at the sound of bone hitting bone.

"How does that feel, asshole?" Jaxon proceeded to pound Richard's face without mercy.

Zora scrambled for shreds of clothes to cover herself, but then she grew alarmed at the continuous pounding by Jaxon on the now whimpering Richard. "Jaxon," she yelled as she climbed up onto her trembling legs. She had to stop him before he actually killed the man.

"Jaxon, stop. He's not worth it." She placed a hand against his shoulder and continued to call his name. Blood painted her hardwood floors. "Please, Jaxon. Please, stop," she sobbed.

Jaxon had no qualms about killing Richard and catching a case. He had pure fire boiling in his blood and a snarl curling his lips. But it was Zora's tears that finally did it. Jaxon stiffened and stopped a punch in midair. His chest heaved from the sheer strength it took to restrain himself.

He stood up, looked at his hands. They were bruised and covered with blood. Richard's. Seconds later, police and the building's security filled the large penthouse.

Jaxon turned and gathered Zora into his arms. When he first heard her screams, fear, like he had never known, seized control of his body. And then seeing Richard on top of Zora...

Jaxon closed his eyes and wished he could block

that memory out of his head forever. But it probably wasn't possible anytime soon. "Are you all right, baby?" he asked in a choked whisper.

"Yes. Thank God you arrived when you did," she sobbed. "I don't know what would've happened." Zora started crying.

"Shhh, baby. It's okay." He squeezed her tight. "Everything is going to be all right."

Zora sighed deeply and she sought the comfort of Jaxon's arms. After a few long minutes, she pulled in a deep breath and tried to put on a brave front. It wasn't working too well. She was trembling like the last fall leaf in the beginning of winter.

"We had a dozen calls about a woman screaming in here," a police officer said. "Is someone ready to tell us just what in the hell happened?"

Richard groaned.

Jaxon kicked him in the leg.

"Hey, hey, hey!" the officer shouted. "Back off. Back off."

Jaxon's angry black stare shifted to the cop.

"Just calm down. And tell us what happened."

Three hours later, Zora was still talking. At least she had been afforded the opportunity to put on some clothes. A pair of sweatpants and a T-shirt. The whole time she was giving her statement, she remained glued to Jaxon's side. Jaxon as well as Billy, the doorman, collaborated on the time line of events.

Zora was still in a daze and couldn't believe how this whole night had transpired. The most humiliating part came when posing for the police photos. Embarrassed, hurt and confused, she had never been in this type of situation before. She had always heard about it, seen it, but never in a million years did she ever believe that something like this could happen to her.

The new reality was that it could happen to anyone at anytime.

It took some convincing, but Zora finally placed a call to her private physician and had him come and check her over. Somewhere around three in the morning, she received confirmation that she didn't have any broken bones. At most, she would have some bruising and some swelling, but for the most part, she was going to be just fine.

Richard was taken into the station and would be booked for aggravated assault. A charge he suddenly begged for her not to press when the gravity of what he'd done had hit him. By morning, it would've hit them all. No way would something like this not hit the gossip tabloids and blogs.

The very thing she didn't need.

At five in the morning, the last police officer left her apartment. She and Jaxon were finally alone.

"Is there anything I can get for you?" he asked, eager and willing to do anything.

"Nah. I'm just going to make myself a compress

with one of those ice packs the doctor left." She started to stand up.

"No. No. Sit back down," he insisted. "I'll do it." Jaxon was on his feet in a flash. Jacketless and tieless, he rolled up the sleeves of his shirt and got to work. The whole time, he started beating himself up. He should have been here sooner. He shouldn't have allowed her to go home with that asshole— though admittedly, he never knew Richard possessed such a violent side.

Jaxon shook his head. He never understood men who beat up women. It was such a sinister way to exact power. Such things didn't make them more of a man, it made them more of a monster. Compress in hand, Jaxon returned to Zora's side in the living room. "Here we go."

"Thanks." She swiped at a tear and then pressed the cool compress against her left cheek.

"Baby, I'm so sorry," he said as his eyes filled with tears. "This should've never happened."

"Don't." She shook her head. "This is *not* your fault."

"It's just—"

"Let's not talk about it anymore," she said, her eyes pleading with his. "I'm just happy you came when you did."

Jaxon leaned forward and planted a kiss against her bruised, soft lips.

She smiled and then settled into the crook of his arm.

He pressed another kiss on top of her head and allowed a few stray tears to drip into her hair.

"Jaxon?"

"Yes, baby?"

"Stay with me tonight?" she asked in a small voice.

He nodded. "Absolutely."

Chapter 17

Zora slept like a baby.

She had one of those dreams she couldn't remember, but she woke up feeling comfort and love. She drew in a deep sigh and uncurled and stretched her body as far as she could. When she bumped into something hard, her eyes sprang open wide and her heart leaped up into the center of her throat.

At the sight of Jaxon, nestled in her baby blue silk sheets, a tender smile touched her lips. Then the pain arrived. She could feel the whole left side of her face throb in double time, while the mental list of why and how such a thing like last night happened picked up just where it had left off.

But…watching Jaxon sleeping had a calming effect on her. He still had on his suit pants, but sometime during the night, he must've stripped out of his shirt, shoes and socks. It still took her breath away at how heartbreakingly handsome he was. And now he was her personal hero—her very own knight in shining armor.

Zora's greedy gaze took in the span of his broad chest and perfectly chiseled abdominals. This was not the body of a man who worked behind a desk. This was a work of art by a man who took care of himself and right now she appreciated his dedication.

Spellbound, Zora reached out and gently touched him. Softly, she stroked her hands along his silky skin, loving the feel of it on her fingertips. His muscles quivered like lazy waves rippling across a still pond. For a long while she was content with this game, but then she wanted to expand her exploration so she allowed her fingers to roam from the valley of his abs up to the mountain peak of his right breast nipple. Once there she drew lazy circles.

Jaxon sucked in a long breath before his eyes fluttered open. "Don't you know it's not fair to torture a man this early?"

"Hey," she whispered as she stretched up his long body and pressed a kiss against his plump lips. "FYI—we fell asleep early this morning, I suspect that it's probably closer to evening by now."

Jaxon frowned as he turned his head toward the

window. True enough it was closer to evening than morning. "We slept the whole day away?"

"I think we kind of deserved it."

His lopsided grin told her that he agreed. "How do you feel?"

"Pretty beat up," she admitted. "But I'll survive. How do I look?"

Jaxon's smile stretched wider. "Beautiful."

She laughed. "You are such a *good* liar."

He simply shook his head. "No. Nothing can touch the beauty that I see." He kissed the tip of her nose. "Nothing."

Zora's heart sped up as if she'd just been given an electric jolt. "I'm glad you're here."

"There's no other place I would rather be." He gently cupped her face in his hands and then kissed her as if she was the most precious thing in the world to him. Behind his tender kiss raged a passion and desire that overwhelmed Zora and she moaned as if drunk by its potency.

Wanting more, she slid her arms up his smooth chest and locked them behind his head.

He pressed closer, but held back as if he was afraid that he would hurt her.

His thoughtfulness only deepened what she was feeling. She unlocked her arms so she could drive a hand back down his body to cup the erection straining against the seam of his pants.

Jaxon jumped as if she'd stabbed him.

"What's the matter, baby?" she asked puzzled.

"Nothing. It's just that…" He smiled tenderly into her eyes. "I'm just surprised, that's all. We don't have to do that right now. You should rest," he urged.

The last thing Zora wanted to do was throw water on the fire that was raging in her. "It's okay," she whispered against his lips. "I want to." She gave his cock a hard squeeze.

He still held back. "Are you sure, baby?"

Another squeeze. "I'm positive," she said, staring into his eyes. "I need you now. Make love to me."

Despite her reassurance, Jaxon hesitated, but then finally gave in to the powerful force bursting from his chest. With delicate care, he shifted his weight and rolled her over onto her back.

Zora helped him lift her T-shirt up and over her head. Her full, round breasts bounced and jiggled free beneath him.

Jaxon groaned at just the sight of them. He scooped one into his large hand and filled his ravenous mouth with the other.

Zora sighed while her body seemed to melt into the bedding. She closed her eyes while wave after wave of desire crashed against her inner shores. What was it about this man's mouth that drove her insane? Whether it was his kisses or his hypnotic suckling, he possessed some magical power that left her weak and wanting.

Still feasting like a starving animal, Jaxon abandoned one taut nipple for the taste of the other one and found it equally delicious.

Zora tossed her head among the silk pillows as she sank deeper into a pool of pleasure. When she felt his hands on the waistband of her sweatpants, she was convinced that she was just seconds from drowning in that same pool. Somehow, she managed to lift her hips so he could peel her pants and panties from off her hips.

Jaxon's mouth fell away from now glossy nipples, but trekked a trail of wet kisses down her body.

Zora writhed beneath him while her breath thinned in her chest.

"Spread your legs," he whispered, pressing a kiss against her black, springy curls.

Gracefully, Zora slid her legs east and west so her body's hidden treasure was before his lustful eyes. "So beautiful. Open it up for me, baby."

Without hesitating, Zora slid her hand between her legs and spread her thick lips wide.

Jaxon groaned at the sight of her stiff clit glistening like a bright pink pearl. Sometimes though, Jaxon liked to play with his food. So instead of just plunging in, he gently eased one finger in her wetness and then smiled at how it slipped and glided around inside.

"Awww." Zora sighed and cupped her breasts.

"You like that, baby?" he asked, dipping in a second finger.

"Oh, yes," she moaned and then bit down on her lower lip.

"I'm liking it, too." He kissed her inner thigh. "Listen to your body, baby." He stroked deeper. "Hear that?"

"Ssss, baby." He sucked in a deep breath and then rained kisses all along her inner thighs. "Can I have some of your candy, baby? Hum?"

"Y-yes!" she panted as she squeezed the tips of her nipples.

"Thank you, baby," he praised and then uncurled his long tongue around the tip of her clit.

Zora sighed, quivered and gasped. If she thought she was going to get a moment to try and collect herself, then she was sadly mistaken. Jaxon removed his fingers and plunged his tongue in deep and then wiggled his way to her pulsing G-spot. Automatically her hips lifted off the bed and her mind emptied of all thoughts.

Two seconds later, Zora grabbed a fistful of the bed's silk sheets and an explosive orgasm splintered her body into a million pieces and then miraculously put her back together again.

Jaxon continued his wild feasting while Zora tried to lock her knees behind his head and pull away. But he was having none of that. He easily pushed her legs back down and kept her locked in front of him.

"Wait, wait," she panted. She needed to try and catch her breath.

But he didn't wait—he couldn't wait. He needed and wanted more from her. He continued lapping up her creamy candy like a man addicted to sugar.

"I can't. I can't. I—" Jaxon's tongue slapped against her clit just right and Zora's eyes sprung wide as her next orgasm hit with the force of an atomic bomb.

"That's it." He popped his mouth off her clit and slid his fingers back in while wave after glorious wave rippled through her.

Zora tugged so hard on the sheets that they came loose from two of the four corners. When the world finally settled around her, Jaxon had peeled out of his pants and was rolling on a condom.

"Wait," she said.

He looked up at her.

"I haven't had the pleasure of tasting you yet," she said.

A smile exploded across Jaxon's face. "All you had to do was ask." He hopped back onto the bed.

Zora grinned and instructed him, "Lay back."

Jaxon stretched back against the pillows and folded his arms behind his head so he could watch the show. And what a show.

She smiled and then swirled her tongue around the head of his thick shaft.

"Oh, damn." He chuckled. "I didn't know you could get down like that."

Zora relished the compliment by sinking her

million-dollar lips down the length of his long shaft. She took in a good three-quarters without gagging and then bobbed back up again.

"Sssss. Oh, baby." He unfolded one arm so he could lazily roam his fingers through her hair while she sucked and suckled like he was a candy cane. But when he felt his toes begin to curl, he sat up to take over.

"Chicken," she teased, knowing that he'd deliberately stopped her from making him come.

"I'll show you chicken." He winked as he rolled on his condom. "How do you want it, baby?"

Excited, Zora climbed onto her knees.

"Hmm." Jaxon kissed her on her round ass. "Doggy-style." He moved up behind her and then took his time easing the head of his cock into her slick walls. "Ssss. Damn, you're so tight."

No. You're so big. Zora closed her eyes as her mouth sagged open.

Jaxon grabbed her hips and continued to sink deeper. When he was finally all the way in, she couldn't speak. Then he started to stroke—and she felt as if she was losing her mind.

He rocked her body deep and hard, loving the sight of her ass sliding and slapping against his body. A few times he sat back on his legs and watched her as she took over and backed everything she had up on him. "That's it. Show me how much you like this dick."

Smack. Smack.

"Damn, I love how you feel," he hissed. Soon he could feel her inner walls quake all around him and he lost control. "I'm gonna come," he panted and then "Awww." He tried to still her hips, but Zora decided to give him a taste of his own medicine and continued to throw her ass back up against his dick until his whole body started to vibrate.

"You like that, baby," she taunted him.

Jaxon laughed and pulled out. "You think your ass is funny," he said and flipped her onto her back and then slid on a new condom.

Zora squealed when he retaliated by tickling her.

"You think that shit is funny?"

Being extremely ticklish, Zora laughed and giggled uncontrollably.

"Well, I tell you what— I got something for you." With one good, smooth stroke he was buried back deep into her silky walls.

"Aah." Zora's eyes rolled.

"Um, hmm. You're not laughing now, are you, baby?"

"N-no."

Jaxon added a couple of slow grinds to prove his point. "You like this dick?"

"Oooh, yeah." Her hips joined in on the action.

"That's right, baby. Sssss. Is this my pussy?"

"Y—y-y—"

"I can't hear you." *Smack. Smack. Smack.* "Tell me whose pussy this is."

"Y-yours. Awww."

"That's right. Let me show you how much I love my pussy." With that, Jaxon took her legs and folded them over her head. Then his hips turned into a human jackhammer.

The sounds that came out of Zora's mouth were nonsensical, but Jaxon loved hearing it all the same. Soon, Zora bucked and moaned while she was coming all over the place.

Jaxon wasn't too far behind. "Oh, yeeeesssss." A white light blinded him and he rolled over and collapsed on the bed beside her. After pulling in a few deep breaths, he peppered kisses across her brow. "God, I'm so glad I found you."

"You mean that?" she asked, staring up into his face.

"Absolutely." He cupped her face like a delicate piece of china and then kissed her with all the emotions he was feeling inside. When he finally pulled back, a dreamy expression covered Zora's face.

"Hmmm. Nice," she whispered and wrapped her arms around his waist. "I do have one question I need to ask."

"Okay."

"Now, I want you to really think about this before you answer."

"Sounds serious."

"It is serious."

"All right." He braced himself. "What is it?"

"Jaxon Landon, will you go out with me?"

A deep rumble of laughter erupted from Jaxon's chest. "Zora Campbell, I thought you would never ask."

Chapter 18

"Thank you for calling the Platinum Society, this is Jessica. How may I help you?" No sooner had she answered the phone did she glance up and see Zora entering the house. "What? Sir, we are *not* that kind of service." She rolled her eyes and slammed down the phone. "I swear we get at least one of those a day," she muttered under her breath. "Zora! How nice to see you."

"Hi, Jess. Is Melanie here?"

"Did someone call my name?" Melanie sing-songed and she blew into the office, carrying a stack of folders. "Jessica, will you make sure to tell Veronica to process these new applications?"

"Will do," Jessica said, reaching for a pen.

"And how are we doing with tonight's party? Is everything still on schedule?"

"So far so good. Vincent had to drag our little millionaire playboy to the barber shop this morning. He put up a good fight about cutting off those dreads."

Melanie rolled her eyes. "It's so hard to get these spoiled playboys to put in any kind of effort."

Zora smiled as she silently agreed with her.

"Now to what do I owe the pleasure of this visit?" She reached out and rubbed a hand up and down Zora's right arm. "How are you doing, sweetie?"

"Doing great." Zora swallowed. "If memory serves me right, it's my turn to take you out to lunch."

"Ooh?" Melanie glanced down at her watch. "I can always squeeze in a free meal." She winked. "Jessica, call me on my cell if you need anything."

"Yes, ma'am."

Fifteen minutes later, they were seated around a wrought-iron table at a Sag Habor café. When Zora removed her large sunglasses and set them on the table, she didn't miss the subtle way Melanie scanned her face.

"The swelling and bruises went away two weeks ago."

"And the bruises on the inside?"

"I had a little help getting rid of those," Zora admitted.

"Zora, I—"

"Don't." She shook her head. "You had nothing to do with it. The only person to blame for that night is Richard. He and he alone—no matter what they print in the paper."

In the three weeks since Richard's attack, her assistant and publicist went out of their way to keep most of the trash that was being printed away from her. But it proved to be impossible when she returned to work. Whether it was makeup artists, interviewers or even visiting the people at the labs for her skincare line. Everyone was whispering, leaving copies of gossip rags lying around everywhere.

Anyone and everyone felt free to comment about her life. It was a whole new realm for her and everyone seemed shocked to see the door on her privacy blown completely off. Luckily she had someone like Jaxon to shoulder her through the storm.

On the flip side, she heard rumors of Richard losing his job and then disappearing altogether. As long as he showed up for his court date, Zora just said *good riddance.*

Melanie plucked a shrimp from her cocktail. "So…you and Jaxon?"

Zora had prepared herself for an I-told-you-so moment with Melanie, but she still blushed like a girl having her first crush. "Go ahead. Get it out of your system. *Maybe* you were right."

Melanie's left brow arched. *"Maybe?"*

Zora rolled her eyes.

"Zora, Zora, Zora. When will you learn that when it comes to matters of the heart, I'm *always* right?"

"Don't break your arm trying to pat yourself on the back."

"If I don't do it nobody will." She winked. "Sooo. Tell me all the juicy details."

"Well." Zora drew in a deep breath. "We've just been *chillin'*—hanging out. You know."

Melanie rolled her eyes. "Fine. Don't tell me."

"Tell me something," Zora said, picking up her glass of lemonade. "How did you know?"

"What do you mean?"

"Jaxon and I. How did you know that we would...hit it off?"

"Oh, that's easy," Melanie said. "Jaxon Landon, whether he'd admit it or not, is a lot like his grandfather. Hard—but loyal. He's motivated, success-driven, generous, reliable...just like you."

Zora smiled.

Melanie reached a hand across the table. "I'm glad that that bastard did hasn't caused any permanent damage—physically or psychologically. He deserves everything that's coming to him."

"Thank you."

"You know, Zora, I've been proud of you for a looonnng time. When I approached you about Jaxon, it really was because I was concerned that while you were chasing professional success, that you forgot that you deserved success in your personal life, as well." Melanie's gaze fell. "We all have to remind ourselves of that, I guess."

Zora stared at her friend and knew that she was thinking about her deceased husband. But a second later, the clouds parted and Melanie's smile returned. "Well." She drew in another deep breath. "Let's not celebrate too early. We still have to get you married."

"Married?"

"Yes, *married.* I have a reputation, you know."

"Damn, man, I haven't seen you in ages," Dale said as Jaxon approached the lunch table.

The men stopped and gave each other a half-shoulder greet. "Three weeks isn't such a long time."

"Three weeks is three years in dog years," Dale said. "Should I pretend not to know why I haven't seen your ass down at the Velvet Rope?"

Jaxon settled into a seat with a smile as big and wide as Texas. "Aw, man, you know how it is. Work. Work. Work."

"I'm not talking about your nine-to-five job, man. I'm talking about that supermodel you were moaning about a while back."

Their waiter appeared.

"My usual," he ordered.

"Yes, sir. A double Scotch and the seafood risotto coming right up," the waiter recited.

"Well, good to know that not everything is changing about you," Dale said.

"Yeah. You still got jokes."

"Ha-ha." He scooched up in his chair. "Naw, for real though, man. Are you and Zora Campbell an item?"

"Why, are you writing a column?"

"C'mon, man. You and her are splashed everywhere—especially after you opened a can of whoop-ass on Richard Myers. Not saying that his ass didn't deserve it. I know the next time I see him, I have a left and a right hook for him to meet."

Jaxon's jaw hardened just at the mere mention of Richard's name. "All I know is that if I *ever* see him again, there's definitely going to be a misunderstanding."

Dale nodded. "I don't blame you. One thing I detest is men who get their rocks off beating up on women—for *any* reason."

Jaxon bobbed his head in agreement, but was ready to talk about something else.

The waiter returned with his drink.

"Thank you," he said with a tip of his head.

"Sooo?" Dale waited.

"Sooo—what?"

"Come on, man. Don't play me. Is it true or not?"

Jaxon fought but failed to keep a smile from curling the corners of his lips. "You know you shouldn't always believe what you read in the papers."

"Aww. It's like that?"

"A gentleman never kisses and tells," Jaxon informed him.

"Since when?" Dale laughed. "Wasn't it you just cryin' in his Scotch about a month ago, talking 'Oh, Dale. I don't know what I'm gonna do. There's sparks sparking all over the place.'" He waved a finger in Jaxon's face. "Wasn't that you or do I have you confused with some other cat?"

Jaxon laughed until he had tears rolling down his face.

"C'mon, man. You know you're my idol. Throw this old dog a bone."

"All right. All right." He tossed up his hands. "I give up. You got me. I have been spending a lot of time with Zora."

Dale crossed his arms and leaned forward. "Yeah?"

"Yes. And that's all I'm saying. No details."

Dale frowned. "Oh, God."

"What?"

His old friend shook his head as he took a sip of his drink. "Anytime a man doesn't want to give details it means that the shit has gotten serious."

Jaxon shrugged and went for his own drink.

"Aww, man. Aww, man. You just got out of one fake relationship, you don't need to dive into another one."

"Very funny."

"It's not funny," Dale said. "It's serious—too damn serious if you ask me. The last thing you need to be doing is falling in love."

"What?" Jaxon jerked his head around as if afraid that anyone had overheard the *L* word. "Keep your voice down."

"Uh-huh." Dale nodded as if he already knew the truth. "No offense, Jaxon, but uh…you're not exactly the marrying type."

Jaxon drew up his chin. "Offense taken."

"What—I'm wrong? Is that what you're saying?"

"What I'm saying is…" Jaxon lowered his voice. "Is…that I think I've finally found the one."

Dale shook his head. "Don't do it, man. Don't do it."

Jaxon's irritation started to take hold.

"There's a reason why you hang out with an old cat like me."

"Really?"

"Yeah—for the wisdom."

Jaxon's laughter returned. "Oh, is that right?"

"Exactamundo." Dale pushed his drink aside. "The lifestyle we lead—with all the money, power and beautiful women?" He shook his head. "The game is too strong and the temptation is too much. I know. I love my wife and it breaks my heart every time I cheat on her."

Jaxon rolled his eyes. "No offense, you and I are two different people."

"Offense taken," Dale volleyed. "Have you really thought about this—a relationship with a celebrity? I mean, you're somebody in the financial world, that'll get you on the cover of three, four magazines tops! Dating somebody like Zora Campbell will mean photographers in the garbage can. Hell, in just the couple of weeks since you two have been an item, I've read some stuff that I never knew before. Like why didn't you tell me that you like Cocoa Puffs for breakfast?"

"What?" Jaxon rolled his eyes. "I've never touched the stuff."

Dale snapped his fingers. "See what I mean? If these people can't find anything, they'll make things up."

Jaxon waved off that nonsense. "Since when have you known me to care about what other people think?"

"You're missing the point."

"Maybe it's a ridiculous point," he countered.

"Even if people are talking about the rift between you and your grandfather?"

Jaxon stiffened and then returned to again waving off the comment. "So what? Who cares?" But he did care a little bit. True it hadn't been a great secret that he and the old man struggled to get along, but it did feel a little weird to think the whole matter would be splashed across the papers like a public drama.

"Uh-huh."

Their lunch arrived and for a few seconds, their thoughts returned to their respective corners. However, no sooner had the waiter stepped away, Dale opened his mouth.

"Dating a model every now and again is fine, but—"

"Stop." Jaxon held up a lone finger and impaled Dale with a sharp look. "Look, I know that we're *boyz* and all, but I'm going to have to ask you to shut up."

Dale snapped his mouth shut.

"Now, I'll admit that life in the fast lane means fast money, lots of power and a different woman every night. But there comes a time when *boyz* put away their toys in order to become men. I've made my money. I've wielded power and yes, I've had my share of women, but something is missing. It has been missing for a long time. I just didn't know it. And now that I've found it, I'll be damned if I'm going to sit here and let you try and convince me to throw it all away. I already have my own list scrolling through my head about why this can't work out, but what you need to understand is that despite that list, I'm going to do everything I can to *make* it work. She's different. I've only known her for a short while, but in that time I feel more alive now than I have in a *very* long time.

"Now, Dale, I consider you a good friend. We have had plenty of laughs together, but if you're not on board with where I'm headed with this relationship, then I'm going to have to ask you to get off the damn train."

Jaxon and Dale's gazes locked for a long minute.

Dale eased all the way back into his chair. "So it *is* like that?"

"I'm afraid so."

After a few more seconds, Dale's lips split into a large grin. "Well, it's about damn time."

Chapter 19

Jaxon wouldn't tell her where they were going for their first *official* date. He just told her to be dressed and ready to go by seven. Their date would have been sooner, but Zora had been self-conscious about her injuries and the strange places cameras would pop up. So for the past three weeks they elected to stay hidden at either her or his place.

Not to say that they didn't have some terrific evenings. Jaxon had the best of everything catered to wherever they were—complete with a waitstaff, flowers and once even a violinist. Turns out, Jaxon was a secret romantic.

And in the bedroom, he was ten stars—off the charts.

He was a great listener. When she talked about her childhood, college or even her old modeling heydays, he truly listened and asked questions. One thing she shouldn't have done was tell him her childhood nickname: Frog Legs.

Now, *he* teased her about it.

In return, Zora returned the favor. She listened to fun and wonderful stories about his parents. It sounded to her like Jaxon suffered from survivor's guilt. He hadn't been there when the criminals had broken into his parents' home; ordinarily he would've been. Maybe—just maybe he'd picked up his father's battles as his own. The battle that never had a chance to end between Carlton and his son.

But Zora sensed that he wasn't ready to hear that—not yet anyway.

"You should forgive him," she had told him one night, lying in his arms.

Jaxon stiffened and fell silent.

Zora took a chance and continued. "The fighting is not going to get you anywhere. If it could, you'd be there by now. Look at it from Carlton's point of view."

"Oh, God, not you, too."

"No. Listen. Even if you're right and your grandfather drove your father away. Think about what his death is doing to Carlton. Don't you think he's beating himself up just as much?"

Jaxon didn't respond.

"I'm not trying to tell you what to do. We're all learning that there's no manual to life—therefore we're all going to make mistakes. We're all going along, trying to do the best we can in the little time that we have."

Silence.

"Just think about it."

Jaxon finally smiled, kissed her and then made sweet love to her. And they hadn't spoken about him and his grandfather since.

Zora's doorbell rang, jarring her out of the memory. She had been ready a full hour early and literally raced to answer her front door. Her expectations were rewarded at the sight of Jaxon standing on the other side of the door, holding a single white lily.

She gasped. "My favorite. Aww. You remembered."

"Of course. I remember everything about you." He took a moment to drink in her profile. The black one-shoulder Versace dress hugged her curves like nobody's business. "I must say, Ms. Campbell, that dress sure does know how to wear you."

Zora laughed. "So *now* can you tell me where we're going?"

"Sorry." He shook his head. "It's going to be a surprise."

Jaxon escorted her down to the limousine with Kwan standing at the ready.

"Good evening, Ms. Campbell," the young driver gushed.

"Evening." She climbed into the limo.

Jaxon climbed in after her and then swung his arm around her shoulders and pulled her closer. "Are you excited? Our very first date."

"Extremely." Zora laughed. "It was a long time coming."

"Hey, it's not my fault. I asked you out six weeks ago."

"Yeah, but we were supposed to go out two months ago."

Jaxon frowned. "What do you mean?"

Zora suddenly remembered herself. She had never told Jaxon that he was supposed to have been her date the night they met because she'd promised Melanie. Given what she knew now, she wasn't too sure how he would take the news. He didn't like his grandparents meddling in his affairs and somehow paying fifty thousand dollars for a matchmaking service sounded like big-time meddling.

"Oh, nothing." She waved off his question. "Forget it."

"Getting your men confused?"

"Hardly."

Jaxon's frown deepened as if he detected she was hiding something from him. "I guess it doesn't matter." He tried to smile again. "We're together now." He leaned down and pressed his hot mouth against hers.

And just like that, whatever the hell they were talking about was forgotten.

However, the date was a disaster.

At first Jaxon tried his best to keep their destination a secret. An hour later, when he finally pulled his attention from Zora's delicious lips and lush curves, he decided to check in with his driver. "Kwan, is there a problem?" he asked as the tinted glass partition slid down.

"Uh, no, um…" Kwan's head started darting around. "I think we're finally back on the right road."

"You think?" Jaxon's buttery baritone dipped lower.

"No. No. I'm pretty sure now, boss."

But he didn't *sound* sure.

Clearly Jaxon didn't buy it, either, because he quickly extracted his arm from Zora's shoulder and decided to look around, but whatever "right" road they were on was too dark for him to distinguish for himself. "Kwan, what did you do?"

The young driver cringed and then launched into a long, rambling almost incoherent explanation that amounted to him not following the specific directions Jaxon had given.

Jaxon was heated and he was trying his best not to just curse the boy out.

Zora pressed a hand to Jaxon's shoulder and encouraged him to calm down.

"It's ruined," Jaxon hissed under his breath, glancing at his watch. "By the time we reach the airport…if we get to the airport…" He cut himself off and shook his head. "I knew I should have been paying attention. That boy can get lost in a broom closet."

Zora sympathized with him. Clearly Jaxon had put a lot into whatever he'd planned and he was taking Kwan's incompetence hard. Minutes later, and to no one's surprise, they weren't on the right road—that became clear when the pavement ended and the trees thickened and multiplied.

Jaxon barked for the driver to pull over. On the side of the road, he apologized to Zora and then went to climb behind the driver's wheel himself. Next clue that told them that they were good and lost came at the discovery that the limousine's GPS system wasn't working or couldn't find a signal.

Jaxon's mood turned black and Kwan, perhaps in fear for his life, stopped rambling endless excuses.

Torn between feeling sorry for the boy and concerned about their surroundings, Zora thought it was best for her to just let Jaxon handle whatever mess they were in. However, there was very little that he could do since right about that time the limo ran out of gas.

"I don't believe it," Jaxon decried.

Zora had to agree, especially when she realized that it had been a long time since she'd seen another car. Everyone checked their cell phone and found that just like the GPS, none of their cell phones were picking up a signal.

A thousand knots looped and tightened in the pit of Zora's stomach. This whole evening had all the hallmark signs of a bad horror movie. The next plan was to sit it out and wait for a car to show up on the horizon. Jaxon apologized again and then hopped out of the vehicle, giving Kwan the order to stay with Zora.

An hour later, Jaxon returned—without help.

The next and only plan left to them was for all of them to walk and try to find a gas station, a store or something. The problem with that great big idea was that Zora was hardly wearing the type of shoes to go hiking in.

But what choice did she really have?

Jaxon tried to help by offering her his shoes, but what good would it really do for her to slide her size-nine foot into a men's shoe size fourteen?

"Maybe I should just go alone and leave you and the kid here?" Jaxon suggested. "It would be faster."

Zora didn't like that idea. She had very little confidence that Kwan, bless his heart, could protect her out there in the boondocks if something was to happen. "No," she insisted. "We'll all go together."

Thirty minutes later, Zora wished that she could just chop off her feet and be done with it. Her feet may have looked cute, but her dogs were barking like nobody's business. Jaxon picked up on her misery and surprised her by reaching over and swooping her up into his arms. She wanted to protest and insist that he didn't need to carry her, but she was too thankful and relieved to utter such nonsense.

But soon her bladder started protesting. She tried to hold it in and then told herself to try not to think about it, but her bladder refused to be ignored. "Jaxon, I—I gotta pee."

"Come again?"

"I—I'm sorry, but I gotta pee."

Jaxon and Kwan stopped. Everyone looked around. There wasn't much around, but what was around didn't exactly look safe for a woman to go traipsing through to go tinkle.

"Are you sure?"

"I don't have a choice," she informed while trying to squeeze her thighs together. "I gotta go."

Jaxon sighed and set her back down. They both looked at the tall, dead grass off on the side of the road with trepidation. But unless Zora wanted to embarrass herself and ruin her dress, she needed to get moving. Gathering her courage, she took a deep breath and raced into the grass. However, at the sound of it crunching and scratching up against her legs, she ran right back out.

"Come with me."

Jaxon's black mood cleared a bit at watching her hop from one leg to the other.

"Please?"

"As you wish, ma'am." He glanced at Kwan. "You think you can manage to stay put?"

Kwan hung his head. "Yes, sir."

Zora grabbed Jaxon by the hand and pulled him with her into the tall, brown grass. She didn't go too far, just far enough to do what she had to do. "Turn around."

Jaxon chuckled. "What?"

She was hopping and hiking up her dress. "You heard me. Turn around."

"Why? I've already seen you naked," he complained, but did as she asked.

"It's not the same thing and you know it." She rolled her panties down and then held them by the crotch when she squatted. The relief she felt was like its own kind of orgasm and she couldn't help but moan.

Jaxon laughed and rocked on his heels.

"Stop laughing. It's not funny," she pouted, but she was unable to keep the bemusement out of her own voice.

"It's a *little* funny," he said.

"Uh-huh." She kept peeing. "So do you think now that you can tell me where you were taking me this evening or is it still some big secret?"

He hesitated while his shoulders deflated. "I was taking you to Quench."

"Aww. That place is fabulous." She sighed. "And I haven't been there in ages." She paused. "But isn't that in Sag Habor?"

"Yeah. I should've known better than to take my eye off Kwan's driving. The man is direction-challenged."

"So why does he work for you?"

"Tell me and we'll both know." He rolled his eyes and then asked, "Damn, what all did you have to drink?"

"Ha-ha. Very funny. I— What was that?" Zora jumped and snatched her panties up, thinking she heard something rustling in the grass.

Jaxon turned around. "What was what?"

Zora didn't know and didn't care to stick around to find out. She wiggled her dress down, snatched Jaxon's hand and took off running damn near all at the same time. At the sight of them hauling tail, Kwan's eyes bugged out and he started running himself.

"Whoa, hold up, Kwan," Jaxon barked.

The young man kept going, but he slowed down a bit as he glanced over his shoulder.

"Where in the hell are you going?" Jaxon thundered, trying to suppress a laugh.

Since they were now back on the main road, Zora had also slowed down—though her heart still raced like a thoroughbred. "Oh, my God," she kept repeating until she finally stopped and bent over at the waist to catch her breath. "I almost died back there."

Jaxon laughed. "I highly doubt that."

"You don't know. You didn't see it," she said defensively.

"Did *you* see it?" he asked. His eyes sparkled and danced beneath the full moon.

"Well…not exactly," she admitted grudgingly.

Jaxon's laughter roared through the night. When he saw that his reaction bruised her feelings, he quickly wrapped an arm around her shoulders and pulled her close. "Aww, sweetie. I'm sorry." He kissed the top of her head to try and make it better, however, his chest still rumbled with a few extra chuckles. "Don't worry, baby. I got you."

Kwan, finally sensing that there was no danger, stopped running. Yet, he was too embarrassed to walk back toward the couple so he decided to just wait until they caught up with him.

Their walk resumed. Two minutes later, Jaxon swept Zora back into his arms and carried her as if she weighed nothing. Unfortunately, it was another hour before they reached something that looked as if there was remotely any life in it: a run-down motel that probably hadn't had a customer since the early 1980s.

"Under no circumstances are we staying here," Zora said firmly.

Kwan's wide eyes agreed with Zora, but he didn't dare say anything.

"Don't worry, baby. We're just going to use the phone."

The reassurance did little to calm her anxiety. The moment Jaxon pulled the door open to the motel's office, Zora swore that she could see the asbestos leaping into her lungs. When the bell above the door jingled, an elderly white man who looked as though he'd been blessed to see almost an entire century pass, jumped and threw his hands up.

"We ain't got no money here," he proclaimed, cutting to the chase.

Jaxon, Zora and Kwan exchanged looks.

"We just need to use your phone," Jaxon said, setting Zora back onto her feet.

"Huh? Whatcha say?" The old man cupped his ear.

Now, didn't he just hear the bell? Zora thought.

"We need to use the phone," Jaxon repeated.

"Come again?"

"Phone. Can we use the phone?"

"Wait. Let me turn up this damn hearing aid," the old man mumbled. "I swear this sucker ain't worth a damn thing."

Jaxon huffed and shook his head.

"Now, what you say, young man?"

"Do you have a phone we can use?"

The man's face twisted. "Yeah. I got a phone. What the hell are you yelling for?"

Zora snickered. The whole comical exchange seemed to be par for the course that evening. True, none of this was quite what she expected, but she had no doubts that she would remember this night for the rest of her life.

The old man reached under the counter and then plopped down a big, clunky, black rotary phone in front of him. "This ain't gonna be a long-distance call, is it?"

"I don't know," Jaxon said, cutting his gaze toward him. "It depends on where we are."

"I can't have you putting long distance on the phone," the old man insisted.

Jaxon reached inside his jacket pocket and withdrew his wallet. "Don't worry. I'll pay you for it." He slapped down a Benjamin next to the phone.

The old man's face lit up. "I think that'll just about cover it."

It was a long-distance call. And it turned out that Kwan had discovered some forsaken place called Shiba, New Jersey. The town only had a handful of residents, one gas station (that closed a little after sundown) and one motel.

"Hey, don't I know you?" the old man asked, squinting at Zora.

Recognition was the last thing Zora wanted right

now. She shook her head and tried to shy away from the old man. She just wanted this long night to end—hopefully with her back safe and sound in her own bed.

"Yeah, I *do* know you," the old man insisted, wagging a finger at her.

The next thing Zora knew, the guy was producing a glossy tabloid magazine with her picture all big and bold on the cover. In the corner was a picture of Jaxon shying away from photographers as he walked out of her apartment building.

"Now that hardly seems fair," Jaxon joked while he waited on hold. "The left is usually my best side."

Zora smacked him on the shoulder. "Will you just concentrate on getting us out of here?"

"Yes, ma'am. I'm on it."

"Will you sign it for me?" the man stretched a pen toward her. His yellowy smile covered the entire bottom part of his face. "I can't believe it. Two real-live celebrities."

Zora returned his smile and then signed her name. "Here you go."

"Thanks." He took the magazine and then stared at it as if it was a gold mine. "Wait 'til my wife, Mildred, hears about this. Celebrities in Shiba!"

Unfortunately for Jaxon, Zora and Kwan, being in a place that no one has ever heard of made it more than a little difficult to be rescued. No one he talked to could find Shiba on a map. Even Teddy, the old hotel manager, couldn't convince them that Shiba existed.

In the end Jaxon slammed the phone down in disgust. "I can't believe this!" he huffed under his breath.

"Well," Teddy said, shrugging his shoulders. "You're more than welcome to stay the night. I'm sure when Darnell opens the gas station in the morning he could give you pretty good directions on how to get back to the big city."

Stay the night? Zora felt faint.

"Do you think that there's any way we could convince him to open up now?" Jaxon asked.

"You could always ask him." Teddy shrugged.

"Good. Let's call him."

"Can't," Teddy said. "On account he ain't got no phone."

Zora tugged on Jaxon's arm and hissed under her breath, "We're not staying here."

Teddy's hearing aid suddenly became a techno-logical wonder because he overheard Zora's comment. "Here? Oh, good Lord, no. I wouldn't let folks like yourself rent a room here. I was talking about you coming over to me and Mildred's. We're just up a ways. We have plenty of room."

The small gang exchanged looks, but they really didn't have any other options.

"Good. Then it's all settled," Teddy boasted.

Chapter 20

"I'm so sorry that our evening was ruined," Jaxon whispered to Zora as they marched out to Teddy's extended cab pickup truck. "I really wanted to make our first official date something to remember."

Zora laughed. "Don't worry. You accomplished that." She glanced over at him and caught him staring. "Look, don't worry about trying to impress me. That's not what I'm all about. Just know that it's enough for me to spend time with you."

Jaxon stopped when they reached the passenger door. "You really mean that, don't you?"

Zora gazed into a face that she was growing to love. "Absolutely." She leaned up on her toes and pressed a kiss against his soft mouth. "One thing for sure, being around you, life is never boring."

Jaxon chuckled as he stole another kiss. "In that case, you ain't seen nothing yet."

Teddy and Mildred had a nice place.

It was a two-story brick that seemed to be smack-dab in the middle of nothing. Despite the full moonlight, none of them could tell whether the place was a ranch or a farm, but at this point they didn't care, either. They were just all hoping that the place was in better condition than the motel.

When the old motel manager ushered them in, Mildred greeted everyone with a bubbly smile. Zora had never known anyone to be this happy when strangers popped up at your house in the dead of night, looking for a place to stay, but she was certainly grateful to the woman and her husband.

Teddy had called ahead and in the five minutes, Mildred had put on a fresh pot of coffee, warmed up some banana-nut bread and put fresh linens on the beds in the guest rooms. Impressed, Zora couldn't stop thanking the woman for her hospitality.

Mildred blew off all the high praise to do a bit of gushing on her own. She wanted to know everything about the modeling world. Was it as glamorous as it seemed? Did all celebrities have a drug problem? And, of course, would she sign another tabloid magazine that had her picture on it? That rag boasted about a secret love child she was having.

"You know you really shouldn't read that garbage," Zora couldn't stop herself from saying.

Mildred's apple cheeks reddened. "Oh, well. You know I just read it for entertainment. I don't take any of it serious."

Jaxon cleared his throat.

"Oh," Mildred said. "Don't let me go on and on. I'll take you two to your room. It's late and I know you guys ought to be tired."

"You, son, c'mon with me," Teddy told Kwan. "We got a room for you out back."

Mildred beamed at Zora and Jaxon. "You two are staying in the main room upstairs. I got it all fixed up."

Zora fell in step behind Mildred, praying that the room would be as nice as the rest of the house. In truth the place looked as if it should have been one of those Southern bed-and-breakfast places. She didn't have any idea why the couple didn't capitalize on that instead of the run-down motel on the side of road.

"Hmmm. It smells nice up here," Zora realized. She sniffed the air and got a good whiff of something…delicious?

"Here we go." Mildred stopped before the door and grinned at the couple. "This is your room."

Something was up. Zora glanced at the woman's

large smile and dancing eyes and immediately felt that something was going on.

"Aren't you going to open the door?" Jaxon asked.

She looked at him and read nothing. Maybe she was just being paranoid. Zora reached out and turned the knob. But when she pushed open the door—she gasped in surprise at the sight before her. Her gaze first fell on at least a dozen flickering candles and then a small table covered in red rose petals. To the right was a huge king-size canopy bed, draped in all-white linen with another spray of red rose petals.

"I—I don't understand," Zora whispered.

Jaxon moved in close behind her. "Surprised, baby?"

She turned. "Surprised? How did you…you mean this whole—"

"I told you I wanted to make this a night you'd never forget." Jaxon's smile beamed. "A lot of women are impressed with what I can buy them or where I can take them or even…" He nodded toward the bed. "But I don't know of any other woman that would have gone through all of this and still tell me that what matters is spending time with *me*. You're a real class act, Ms. Campbell." He lifted her hand and pressed a kiss against her knuckles. "I'm extremely happy that you're my lady."

Zora tried to blink away her tears but instead

Jaxon kissed them away. And when his lips settled against hers, he intoxicated her senses. She wrapped her arms around him and tried the best she could to fuse their bodies together. But no matter how hard she tried, she couldn't get close enough.

"Make love to me," she whispered raggedly.

Jaxon kicked the bedroom door closed. "What about dinner?"

Zora kicked off her shoes. "We'll eat later. I want you."

Jaxon's jacket and shirt were off in a flash. "God, you don't know what it does to me to hear you say that."

Zora trembled breathlessly as she tried to wiggle her way out of her dress. Jaxon rushed over and helped and then smiled at the sexy black lace underwear she had on underneath.

"Nice."

"I'm glad you approve," she said.

Jaxon's lips lowered to claim hers. In a silent melody, their tongues danced until Zora became dizzy. They fell onto the bed. Their mouths, arms and legs tangled together with desire, passion and urgency. Instead of those feelings lessening with each coupling, they were growing stronger. That fact took both of them by surprise.

For Zora, she didn't think she could ever get used to just the little things that Jaxon did whenever their bodies joined: his warm breath against her neck, his hands skimming along her breasts or even how he moaned her name. Despite it being their first official date, they had passed the stage of hot sex and entered the intimate world of making love.

That place was all new to her. It didn't take her long to relax, get comfortable and enjoy all the new feelings and sensations that were opening up to her. At first it was a lot to take in. With every slow, deep stroke, Zora swore that Jaxon was tearing down the wall around her heart and somehow their souls were blending together. Her breath was not her own.

Jaxon was lost. His mind blown. Nothing in life had ever prepared him for this, but now that he was at the door of love, he was ready to knock the thing down and step inside. Every fiber of his body blended into hers while his hand explored every curve of her breasts and then every contour of her hips. The heat of her mouth left his lips to lick and kiss and nip him everywhere from his collarbone, neck and even his hard nipples.

He damn near came every time his name floated from Zora's lips. He damn near came every time her long fingers glided down his back. And he damn near came every time she thrust her hips up to meet his. But whenever those things happened, Jaxon would hold firm.

Besides, he wasn't so into his own orgasm as he was watching Zora's face in the candlelight whenever she experienced one. The raw, naked emotions that rippled across her beautiful face were like discovering the eighth wonder of the world. Right now he could feel another tremor coursing its way up from the core of her body. Zora emitted a small gasp and lifted her desire-drugged gaze to meet his.

"You coming, baby?"

"Y-yes." Her hands rolled up the curve of his ass and settled on his grinding hips.

"Then let me see it," he said, sinking deeper.

Zora tilted her head, her mouth sagged open, but her gaze remained locked with his as heat rose up and then exploded at the tip of her clit. A cry of ecstasy tore from her lips and her legs locked powerfully behind Jaxon's waist.

Jaxon stiffened and just enjoyed how her silky muscles quivered around his cock. He couldn't describe just how wonderful her body felt—just as he couldn't describe how beautiful she looked all sweaty and kiss swollen.

Somehow he saved up just enough strength so she could roll onto her back and he could take her in her favorite position. He changed it up a bit by letting her remain flat on her back with just her legs spread open for easy entry. He lifted himself up and braced his weight like preparing to do push-ups, but instead rocked up and down into her body with long, powerful strokes.

"Oh, gaaawwwd," Zora moaned, pushing her butt up against his abs. She had come so many times

that she was good and wet, which caused her body
to keep making sucking and smacking sounds. Zora
had to remind herself to breathe, but the task proved
too difficult at the feel of his mouth roaming around
her neck. She squirmed on the bed, her hands grabbing the sheets, pillows and anything else she could
find.

"Oh, Zora, baby," Jaxon panted. "You feel so—
sssssss."

She sensed that he was finally losing control and
took it as her cue to start throwing her ass back at
him as hard as she could manage.

Jaxon stiffened and dropped his knees down in
between her legs. Zora hopped up on hers and continued driving him wild by thrusting backward. "You
coming, baby?" she asked, glancing over her shoulder.

"Hell, yeah," Jaxon hissed through his clenched
teeth. It was his turn for his mouth to sag open and
his body to explode. No doubt that everyone in the
house heard his mighty roar before he collapsed
like dead weight against her back.

He was in heaven.

She was in paradise.

And they were in love.

Chapter 21

"So you're actually taking her to meet your folks?" Dale asked. "Three months and you're ready to jump the broom." He drew a deep breath and dropped down in the empty leather chair in Jaxon's home library. "You certainly don't believe in wasting time."

Jaxon reached out and handed his friend the double Scotch on the rocks he'd requested. "It's like you said. When I see something I want…"

"I know. I know," Dale said, accepting his drink. "Just give me a minute. It's gonna take me some time to wrap my brain around this one."

Jaxon's smile beamed at his friend. "C'mon.

You've been pretending to be happy for me for three months. Don't start wavering on me now."

"That was before I knew I was losing a hanging buddy down at the Velvet Rope. Now I'm stuck looking at Myers's sorry ass trying to drown all his sorrow in a whiskey glass. It ain't pretty. The man has let himself go."

"Glad to hear it."

"That boy got some serious trouble. The SEC is all over his ass. Word is he tried to set Keith Colbert up on some crazy stock package that didn't mount to more than a fancy Ponzi scheme. The man must have been sipping too much Kool-Aid not to know old man Colbert checks things out nine ways to Sunday before he hands over a dollar."

"To tell you the truth, I'm not surprised," Jaxon said. "After that bullshit with Zora, I knew he was capable of anything. It was just a matter of time before he went down."

"Humph! And all these years he's been trying to convince anyone that'll listen that it was you that was knee-deep in insider trading and wild schemes."

"That's what thieves do. It's call projecting," Jaxon said, turning to the chessboard sitting between them. "Game?"

"Yeah." Dale twirled a finger in the air. "Board games instead of beautiful women and lap dances. You're starting to depress me."

"Sorry. No more strip clubs for me," Jaxon announced. "My lady looks pretty damn hot with and without any clothes on. And if I want a lap dance, all I have to do is ask. You should try it with your wife. After all, she used to work the poles."

Dale clapped and rubbed his hands together. "Oh, goody. My very own professional marriage counselor. Next, you'll be telling me that I need to stop drinking and start exercising."

Jaxon tossed up his hands. "All right. I'm going to leave it alone."

"Good."

"I'm just saying monogamy can be a beautiful thing."

Dale huffed out a breath. "Life is never going to be the same, is it?"

Jaxon reached into his pocket and produced a four-carat Cartier ring. "Actually, that's exactly what I'm betting on."

Zora kept messing up her lines on her latest skincare infomercial. She must have issued a thousand apologies to everyone from the key grip to the director. They all cut her some slack—but who knew that love affected someone's ability to concentrate? Hell, it affected her ability to do everything except to smile off in space, bring up Jaxon's name at least fifty times in a conversation and to call or either text message him every other hour.

Everyone knew that she was in love—mainly
because the tabloids reported on it every week. She
had hoped that the whole hoopla surrounding that
would go away; usually people grew bored or sick
of celebrities' complicated love lives and moved on
to the next train wreck. So far that wasn't happening with her.

Of course Todd still loved the renewed attention
in her. It all translated into more sales for her business ventures. Sales were up across the board. Hell,
even Oprah came calling.

Today none of that mattered. The only thing that
Zora could think about was this evening's trip out
to Jaxon's grandparents' estate. She was so nervous
about making a good impression that she worried
whether she would ever get through this infomercial.
Eventually the director called it a wrap and she was
free to go home and obsess over what dress to wear.

If everything went well, Zora hoped to bring
Jaxon to *her* parents' house. It would definitely
shock her parents since they hadn't met a boyfriend
of hers since her high-school senior prom. Then
again, since she had been dating Jaxon, she was
doing a whole lot of things she hadn't done before.

With Jaxon, Zora felt free to be herself. The
supermodel or the businesswoman or the other
dozen things that people expected her to be. And she
made sure to provide the environment so that Jaxon
would feel the same way. On top of the incredible

sex and the deepening love, there was trust and
honesty.

Have you really been honest with him?

Zora's renegade thought caught her off guard and
she froze in the middle of putting on an earring. The
promise to Melanie suddenly lingered in her mind.
Now that she and Jaxon were an item, shouldn't she
tell him that they met because his grandmother had
hired a matchmaking service?

As the second question floated around, she
started shaking her head. A confession like that
didn't bode well for her. Jaxon's pet peeve was his
grandparents' meddling—especially in his personal
life. Was she expected to keep this secret forever?
If so, how could she truly say that there was anything honest about their relationship?

The doorbell rang. Zora looped the last earring
into her ear and rushed to answer the door. To her
surprise, Jaxon wore a pair of casual jeans and a
navy-and-gray Vansport T-shirt. She glanced down
at her Armani ensemble and then back up at him.
"Now, why do I feel overdressed?"

Jaxon laughed as he entered her apartment and
kissed her on her upturned face. "You're meeting
my grandparents, not applying for a job interview."

"I want to make a good impression."

"You have." He pulled her into his arms. "On me.
Isn't that all that matters?"

"Is that right?" She slid her arms around his

neck. "Well, I have to say that you've made quite an impression on me, too, Mr. Landon."

"It took a while," he added.

Zora laughed. "Mmm. Not as long as you might think."

"Aha!" Jaxon smacked her on the ass. "I knew that you were playing hard to get."

"Are you kidding me? When I met you, you had a fiancée."

"We've been over this. It was a joke," he reminded her, rolling his eyes. "I know you don't understand, but trust me, if your parents were always plotting and planning your life, you would take a few drastic measures, too."

"I'm still convinced that they only do what they do because they love you," Zora said. "But you're right. I've never been in your position. My parents have always been supportive of whatever I choose to do—even when they didn't understand my choice. All they ever wanted was for me to be happy. I was lucky. *But* it doesn't mean that your grandparents loved you any less or wanted any more from you. Life doesn't come with instruction manuals."

"I would just settle for them being proud of me," Jaxon said. "I swear to you—not once has Carlton looked me in the eye and said that he was proud of me making my own way in life." His gaze broke contact with her as he shook his head. "I was never really after the money or the accolades or even showing him up. I just wanted Carlton to recognize that I was my own man—that there was a different way of doing things."

Zora felt his pain and pressed closer. "Some men don't know how to say it. Given what you've told me about Carlton, I just think that there's a little more to the story than he's letting on. Even if there isn't, you gotta try to find a way to forgive him and move on." She watched him as he reflected on her words. "Reach out to him. Show *him* how to accept someone for who they are. Maybe then he'll learn how to do the same with you."

Jaxon smiled as he leaned forward and pressed his forehead against hers. "You're something else. You know that, baby?"

Zora shrugged one shoulder and bragged. "I might know a little sumpthin' sumpthin'." She received another playful smack on the ass for that comment. Giggling, she rushed to change clothes.

Jaxon followed and became extremely playful while she tried to make a quick change.

"Will you please stop?" Zora giggled. "I'm trying to get dressed."

"Mmm-hmm." Jaxon eased up behind her and cupped her breasts. "I'm just checking to see if you got these titties safe and secure." He gave them a light squeeze and started nibbling on the back of her neck.

"Jaxoooon," she moaned as she pulled down a folded pair of skinny jeans.

"Hmm?" His hand slid underneath her bra for more skin-to-skin contact. "Looky here. Your nipples are all hard."

A purrlike moan fell from Zora's lips as her mind started to drift off in space.

"Let me just see if these babies taste as good as I remember." He moved around her and dropped his head low to pull her left tit into his mouth. At its cinnamon taste, he groaned out his pleasure and dropped his hand down into her panties. She was already wet and juicy.

Zora dropped the pair of pants she was holding. "Jaxon….we have…to go."

"In a minute, sweetheart," he whispered raggedly. "I'm just going to check out a few things here." He twirled his finger around the head of her clit and then smiled when her legs trembled.

"Baaaaybeeeee…"

Jaxon sank down to his knees and instead of rolling down her Victoria's Secrets, he just moved the crotch of her panties over to the side. "Spread your legs."

Zora forgot her need to get dressed and did as she was told.

"Ooh," Jaxon cooed as if he'd just found a lost treasure chest. He continued to probe his fingers in and out, loving the sight of her juices coating his finger.

Zora leaned back against the wall of her walk-in closet and tried in vain to catch her breath. She nearly came undone when Jaxon looked up with a puppy dog face and asked, "May I have some of this pussy, baby?"

Not able to speak, she just nodded and watched as he leaned forward and his pink tongue slipped inside. "Oh…gawd…that feels good."

Jaxon's tongue plunged in deeper and rotated like a hurricane. In no time at all, ecstasy washed over her and leaked out from the corners of her eyes. "Aah. I'm going to come." Grabbing his shoulders, she let out a thunderous moan. As her orgasmic waves convulsed through her, Jaxon stood up, unzipped his jeans, picked her up and buried himself so deep inside her that another eruption popped off before he even started stroking.

"So wet," Jaxon panted, bobbing her ass up and down his cock.

Zora held on for the ride. She loved how she could feel him almost to her stomach and the sexy faces he made when her ass smacked the base of his dick. Feeling playful, she licked and sucked on his bottom lip.

Jaxon's groans deepened as his hips gained speed. Feeling his peak just on the horizon, he leaned Zora back up against the wall and hammered his hips until he came with so much force that he nearly dropped Zora on the floor. After a minute to catch his breath, he peppered kisses along her collarbone and confessed, "I love you, baby."

Chapter 22

The Platinum Society team beamed smiles at one another as they lifted their champagne glasses high into the air and made a toast. "To another successful union and a satisfied customer," Melanie declared.

"Hear, hear." Veronica, Jessica and Vincent all clinked their glasses together and then drew their first sip of the bubbly drink in sync.

"I gotta hand it to you," Veronica said. "You certainly know how to pair them."

"Of course, young grasshopper," Melanie sassed. "It's in the genes."

"Do we know if he has proposed yet?" Jessica

asked. Her eyes shone like a child's on Christmas morning.

"Not yet. But I got a call from a contact over at Cartier. She said he picked a four-carat stunner."

Veronica shook her head. "It amazes me how you're always the first to know these things."

Melanie playfully tapped Veronica on the nose. "That's my job, sweetheart."

Vincent was a little more reserved. "I don't know. They haven't walked down the aisle yet. And it's not like the man hasn't been engaged before."

Melanie rolled her eyes. "I told you. It wasn't a real engagement. He was just trying to shock his grandparents into backing off. That's all."

"And to prove a point that he was his own man and that he would date and marry whom he chooses," Vincent added, sounding like he was trying to say something without saying it.

Melanie set her champagne down on the bar and folded her arms. "What's your point?"

"My *point* is that his grandmother didn't back off. She hired you."

"Because she knew what was best for him and he was being hardheaded."

"Do you seriously think that's how he's going to see it?" Vincent asked. His gaze swung from his aunt and cousins. "Take it from me. No man likes to be manipulated, and if he *ever* finds out that his grandmother paid a matchmaking service to find him a wife, that's exactly what he's going to think has happened here." He had now successfully ruined the mood.

Internally, Melanie conceded his point. It was a proven fact that when it came to the Landon men, their Achilles' heels were their pride and their stubbornness. "Well," Melanie said, drawing a conclusion. "Then we'll have to make sure that Jaxon never finds out."

Veronica and Jessica agreed with a firm nod and went back to drinking their champagne.

Vincent laughed. "Yeah. Good luck with that."

Sylvia Landon was as happy as a clam, bustling around the house and making sure that everything was in order. Every time she came into a room, the house staff moved faster or scrubbed harder. Even Carlton didn't escape from her micromanaging. After agreeing that he would be on his best behavior, Sylvia also launched into a speech about him not questioning, criticizing or adding his two cents about anything pertaining to Jaxon's professional or personal life. The one rule of the day was: thou shall *not* be argumentative.

"I'm not the one always starting an argument," Carlton complained.

Sylvia rolled her eyes. "I mean it, Carlton. Be on your best behavior."

Carlton may have been used to running a Fortune

100 company with thousands of employees, but at home he knew who was really in charge. "All right. Fine," he said, huffing and rolling his eyes. "I'll keep my mouth shut."

"Perfect." She clapped her hands together.

Wounded, Carlton frowned.

"Aww, baby." Sylvia glided in close and wrapped her arms around his neck. "You know I didn't mean it like that. I just really want this evening to be perfect."

"I know, honey. And I want it to be perfect, too," he said with honest sincerity. "It's not that I *try* to drive him away. You know that, don't you?"

"I do."

Carlton's blue eyes misted. "It always seems to happen. Just like with Junior," he added sadly. "I didn't mean to drive him away—either of them. I just did what my father always did. I was firm, focused and determined that they were always at their best and striving to be the best. That wasn't so wrong, was it?"

"No, baby. It wasn't." She smiled tenderly. "Your heart has always been in the right place. Deep down I believe Jaxon knows this and even thinks that Junior realized it, as well."

Hope sparkled in Carlton's eyes. "You really think so?"

Sylvia sniffed and wiped away a tear. "I do. He had his own son and was coming into his role as a father. Jaxon doesn't remember but there was a lot of head butting going on between him and Junior before that horrible incident." She glanced away, lost in the past for a few heartbeats.

"I wish I could go back," Carlton confessed softly. "There are so many things that I would do differently."

"I know," she said. "There may not be anything we can do about the past, but there's nothing stopping us from doing something about the here and now. Let's just try to accept and support whatever choices he makes in life."

"Like when he claimed he was going to marry that stripper friend of his?" he asked with a crooked smile.

Sylvia groaned and rolled her eyes. "We were talking about you—not me."

Carlton laughed. "The good ol' fashioned double standard."

Sylvia dropped her arms from around his neck and then crossed them against her chest. "I don't know what you're talking about."

"Of course you don't, dear." He kissed her on the cheek and then walked off with a smirk.

When their afternoon delight had drawn to a satisfied end, Zora and Jaxon quickly hopped into the shower, played a little bit longer and then hurried down to the waiting limousine.

"Are you sure there is enough gas in the tank?" Zora asked Kwan, winking.

"Yes, ma'am," he assured her, blushing.

The question had become a standard now whenever he was driving them around. Sure, she had enjoyed the eventful first date, but she certainly didn't want to have to go in the tall, dead grass on the side of the road again anytime soon.

During the long drive out to the Hamptons, Zora and Jaxon remained snuggled up in the back of the limousine. Jaxon wanted to do things but Zora was too scared that Kwan would overhear them.

"C'mon," Jaxon whispered, trying to snake his hands underneath her shirt. "He can't hear or see us. Trust me." He nuzzled sweet kisses along the column of her neck.

She resisted for a while, but she was learning that when Jaxon set his mind on something, he usually got it. In no time at all her feet were pressed up against the ceiling and Jaxon was smothering her moans and sighs with his hot mouth. The long drive seemed to pass by in a blink of an eye to the lovers and then when the vehicle finally rolled to a stop, they bolted upright and frantically tried to get dressed again.

"Oh, my God. I'm going to look like a hot mess when I meet your grandparents."

Jaxon laughed as he zipped his pants. "That, my dear, is something that you will never have to worry about. You'll always look like a million dollars no matter what you have on—" he leaned over and kissed her flushed face "—or off."

"Oh, go on." She smacked him in the arm. A minute later, they climbed out the back of the limousine, touching and clinging to each other the way new lovers always do and not caring what anyone thought about it.

However, Zora was both nervous and giddy—but more from wanting to make a good impression with Sylvia Landon. Given the fact that she was the one who had enlisted Melanie's help in finding the right person for her grandson, she didn't want the woman to run back to Melanie demanding a refund.

"Are you ready?" Jaxon asked.

"About as ready as I'll ever be," Zora admitted and then took a deep breath when Jaxon reached for the door. Once open, they had barely crossed the threshold before Sylvia's lyrical voice floated toward them in greeting.

"You're finally here!"

Zora turned and watched the elegant Sylvia Landon race across the hall and then dive into her grandson's outstretched arms. "Oh, baby. I'm so glad to see you." She pulled out of his arms and then smacked him on the shoulder. "And you're late."

"Ow." Jaxon grabbed his shoulder and pretended to be wounded. "Careful with that right hook, Grans. You might hurt somebody."

Sylvia rolled her eyes at his dramatics. "I've told you for years that you call when you know you're going to be late." She finally turned her gaze toward Zora. "Now, I would know that beautiful face anywhere." She popped Jaxon on the shoulder again. "Introduce me to your friend."

A wide smile hooked across Jaxon's face as he pulled Zora close to him. "Grans, I'd like for you to meet a very special woman in my life, Zora Campbell. Zora, this is the only other woman in my life, my grandmother Sylvia Landon."

"It's nice to meet you," Zora said shyly and stretched out a hand.

"Trust me, dear. The pleasure is all mine." The older woman took her hand and patted it softly.

"I hope I'm not late for the party," Carlton's voice thundered across the spacious mansion as his long strides erased the distance between him and the small group.

Zora remembered Jaxon's handsome grandfather from their sixtieth wedding anniversary, but this time was struck by how, despite the obvious color difference, just how much grandfather and son looked alike.

"Well, now. Aren't you a beauty?" Carlton reached for her hand before being offered an official introduction. "I can see why my grandson has fallen head over heels for you, Ms. Campbell. Next to my Sylvia, you just might be the prettiest thing I've seen in a long time."

Zora laughed. "Well, I certainly know where Jaxon inherited his charm."

The Landons laughed and Zora relaxed. In the next minute, Sylvia latched onto her arm and insisted on giving her a grand tour of the estate. Two hours later, Zora was glad that Jaxon had convinced her to dress casually, because there was no doubt that the high-heeled pumps that she was wearing originally would have been cutting off her circulation by the end of the tour.

All in all, Zora was very impressed with the immaculate home and could tell that Sylvia was very proud of what her husband had been able to accomplish. There was a way that Sylvia lit up when she talked about her husband that made Zora envious, yet it also put her in mind of how her own parents were toward one another. And now when she thought about it, it was exactly how she felt when she thought or talked about Jaxon.

Every time they were together, he made her feel cherished. That was something she had never experienced with another man. Could it be possible that he was the one? The question made her smile because she knew the answer.

At dinner, Sylvia questioned Zora—who couldn't decide whether she felt like she was being interviewed for a federal job or interrogated for a terrorist act. By dessert, both Carlton and Jaxon took pity on her and finally interceded.

"Sylvia, honey. You're going to scare the young woman off before I get a crack at it," Carlton teased.

Embarrassed, Sylvia blushed. "Oh. Forgive me, dear. I guess I just got carried away."

"It's okay," Zora said, relieved for the reprieve.

"Grans means well," Jaxon said, giving Zora a reassuring smile and wink. "She's probably just happy that you don't make your living by sliding down a pole."

"Jaxon!" Sylvia delivered a swift kick to his shin.

"Ow. What am I, your personal punching bag today?" Jaxon laughed.

"Well, you have to admit that was a cruel joke you pulled on us."

"Sorry, but if you asked me, it served you guys right. My life. My decisions."

Zora reached to her right and gave Jaxon's hand a firm squeeze. It was an act of support, yet, a request for him not to start anything.

Jaxon got the hint and pulled back. "Well, I guess it's neither here nor there. I believe I've finally found the one I've been looking for." He picked up Zora's hand and brushed a kiss against her knuckles.

A delicious thrill coursed up Zora's arm and caused a smile to bloom across her face.

Sylvia and Carlton glanced at one another and both knew without a doubt their grandson was in love.

Sylvia reached for her wineglass and tried not to gloat.

Chapter 23

"Melanie, she's perfect," Sylvia declared, clenching the cordless phone against her ear. "And the best part is that Jaxon has fallen for her hook, line and sinker. I couldn't be more pleased!"

"I'm certainly happy to have another satisfied customer," Melanie said. "Given the information that you provided about your grandson, I just knew that Zora was our girl. Though it did start off a little bumpy there."

"You're telling me. Jaxon really had me going with that Kitty character. Not that I have anything against strippers per se—I just don't want them marrying my grandson."

"Per se." Melanie chuckled. "Anyway, I'm just thrilled that it has all worked out. Do we know whether he's proposed yet?"

"Not yet. At least I don't think so. But I can tell it's gonna be anyday now. You should see how he looked at her last night during dinner. He's absolutely crazy about her." Sylvia sighed. "Ah. It all just reminds me of when your grandmother first introduced me to my Carlton. I know that she has to be proud of you."

"That's so kind of you to say," Melanie said. There was a beat of silence and then, "Um. There's just one thing," Melanie hedged.

"Is there a problem?"

"Well…I don't know," Melanie began. "My nephew Vincent brought up something the other day that, in all honesty, does have me a little worried."

"Oookay," Sylvia said, picking up Melanie's anxiety over the line.

"It's just that…if Jaxon ever finds out that you hired a professional matchmaking service, he could construe this whole thing as a form of manipulation and well…given what you've told me about him—" Melanie explained.

"I know where you're going with this, and I agree. I love him but Jaxon is too stubborn and hardheaded for his own good. So he must never find out that I hired a professional matchmaking service. He would absolutely hit the ceiling."

"Good, then we're all on the same page."

"What about Zora? Should one of us tell her not to tell Jaxon?"

"I'll do it," Melanie said. "I'd already told her not to divulge your involvement at the beginning, but she may be tempted, given the status of their relationship."

"Well, that would certainly be a disaster," Sylvia said. "But it has to be encouraging that she has said nothing before now."

"Yeah. But I'll talk to her just to make sure."

"Thanks," Sylvia said, releasing a sigh of relief. "We've come too far to have all this blow up in our faces." After a few more reassurances from Melanie, she quickly said her goodbyes and hurried off the phone. When she turned around to head for the kitchen for her morning coffee, she jumped at the sight of Jaxon standing at her reading-room door. "Oh, my goodness." She pressed a hand against her heart. "You nearly scared me to death!"

"Now, I wouldn't want that now, would I?" Jaxon deadpanned. His eyes were flat and hard.

A small prick of fear pierced Sylvia in the center of her spine. "How long have you been standing there?"

"Long enough." His jaw clenched.

"Oh." Sylvia's mouth went dry and she suddenly had an overwhelming need to sit down.

Jaxon stood there and watched his grandmother as she crept across the room like a tortoise. It was a stark difference from the spry woman who had raced into his arms just yesterday. When she finally settled down into a high-back wing chair, she quietly braided her hands together and waited for whatever explosion that was coming her way.

Jaxon didn't really know where to begin. He was simply coming down to the kitchen to ask the cook if he could prepare and deliver breakfast to his and Zora's room. It was just by chance that he was walking by his grandmother's reading room when he overheard her conversation. "You *hired* Zora to meet me?" he asked, wanting—no—needing clarification.

"No." Sylvia chuckled awkwardly. "I didn't hire *her*. I hired a professional matchmaker. Melanie Harte. She runs this company called the Platinum Society."

Jaxon's head started spinning. "Melanie Harte. Why do I know that name?"

"Oh. You've probably met her. She's usually at all the social functions. Plus, it was her grandmother who introduced me to Carlton. You've met her. You probably just don't remember."

Jaxon had another memory associated with the name. The woman who was waiting outside the bathroom at Cipriani's. Hadn't Zora said her name was Melanie? Jaxon calmly walked over to the chair across from his grandmother and said, "Start from the beginning."

* * *

Zora woke up smiling in a bed that had the softest sheets she had ever slept on. After a night of great conversation and great food, she and Jaxon had retired to one of the guest rooms for a night of great sex. Even now, she relished the pleasurable soreness between her legs. Jaxon had certainly turned her on and turned her out—to the point she kept hearing a voice inside her head say: Mrs. Zora Landon. Each time she heard it, she smiled.

Uncurling in a tangle of sheets, she kept reaching across the bed in search of her lover. Then finally she sat up and glanced around. "Jaxon?" When he didn't answer back, she reluctantly pulled herself out of bed, wrapped the sheet around her body and went to look for him in the adjoining bathroom. But he wasn't there.

Since she was up and already in the bathroom, she decided to go ahead and jump in the shower. If he came back to the room, he could always join her. But twenty minutes later, her lover boy hadn't returned. Zora was disappointed but she really wasn't all that concerned. Maybe he was off finally having that heart-to-heart talk with his grandfather.

She sincerely hoped so. She liked Carlton and could see that the two men really did have a lot in common—in looks and in personalities. She quickly got dressed in another pair of jeans and a T-shirt and set about to see if perhaps there was some breakfast down in the kitchen. However, Zora hadn't taken more than a couple steps outside the bedroom door when Jaxon appeared at the top of the stairs.

Zora smiled, but then her lips quickly curved the other way at the look on Jaxon's face. She was instantly concerned. "What's wrong? Is everything okay?"

"You tell me," he growled, storming toward her.

"Jaxon, come back here." Sylvia's voice snapped at him a second before she also appeared at the top of the stairs.

Zora was confused. "What's going on?"

Jaxon's long strides were coming at her so fast, she was almost afraid that he was about to mow her down. "Tell me about the Platinum Society."

Zora's face drained of color.

"How about Melanie Harte?" Jaxon tried. "Does her name ring a bell?"

Sylvia butted in, "Jaxon, please let me finish explaining."

"No," Jaxon snapped, his patience was clearly just held together by the thinnest thread. "I've heard enough from you right now, Grans. I want to hear Zora's answer."

Zora quickly processed what was going on. Jaxon had found out about Sylvia hiring the Platinum Society to find him a wife—her. "Jaxon, I know what you're thinking."

"How in the hell would you know what I'm thinking?" Jaxon snapped. "Are you going to tell me that you're a mind reader, too?"

"You're upset," she said, trying to talk to him in a calming voice.

"How could you tell, Ms. Campbell? Could it possibly be my angry tone, my tense expression or the fact that my hands are just dying to bounce something up against the wall?"

"Jaxon—"

"How dare you—both of you—try to manipulate me—"

"No," Zora snapped. "That's not how it was."

"Was all of this some kind of sick game—all of it? The whole cat-and-mouse ruse and—"

"No!" Zora started to panic. She could very well lose him over this. "Trust me, I know—"

"Trust you?" he thundered. "Lady, I don't think I even know you."

His words slapped her and she stepped back in shock. "How could you say something like that?"

"How could you *not* tell me?"

Zora drifted to his side to see his grandmother's ashen face. "I made a promise."

Jaxon laughed. "Well, how honorable. You keep your promises."

"It's not like I was *paid* to be with you. A friend asked me—"

"You know what?" Jaxon started backing away.

"I've changed my mind. I don't want to know. I don't want to hear it. I'm just glad I found out before I made the biggest mistake of my life by asking you to marry me."

Zora's heart sank like a stone. "What?"

Sylvia slapped a hand across her heart. "Jaxon, nooo."

Jaxon's eyes misted, but he shook his head as if that would prevent the tears from falling. "I have to get out of here. As usual, these damn walls in this house are closing in on me."

Zora no longer had the will to fight with him. "Then I guess that means that you have to do what you always do—run away."

Jaxon jerked from the verbal blow but then still backed away.

Zora lifted her chin and did a better job in keeping her tears from showing. "Mrs. Landon, would you mind if I had one of your drivers drive me back to the city?"

Sylvia was the only one not ashamed to show her tears. "This is all my fault," she gasped. "Please, won't you reconsider?"

"No. It seems I've already made the biggest mistake of *my* life. I would like to go home now." Without waiting for another word from her glaring ex-lover, she turned on her heel and went to pack her clothes. *Oh, well. It was good while it lasted.*

Chapter 24

For the next two months, Zora threw herself into her work. She did everything she could to block anything that had to do with Jaxon Landon from her mind. Turned out that that alone was a full-time job. But lately she was into this thing where she kept telling herself that she was doing better and so he would be nothing but a distant memory.

Of course it didn't help that the tabloids were back at it, trumpeting from every page that the love affair had crashed and burned. They all speculated on the causes. Some stated that she was still secretly in love with Richard Myers and the others claimed the Jaxon couldn't handle the pressure of living in the spotlight. Zora tried to avoid these rags, but once again, the staff on photo shoots always seemed to leave those gossip magazines in places where she was sure to see them.

Zora's mother grew concerned and now had developed the habit of calling her at least ten times a day to check in on her. She was fine, she kept telling everyone. At least she would be if everyone would just stop asking how she felt.

In the first few days right after the big fight out in the Hamptons, Todd had thought that Zora's sudden zest for work was great. But when sixteen-hour days became twenty-hour days, he grew concerned and just stopped telling her about some of the jobs that were pouring in. And poor Monica started to complain and hint that maybe she needed to start looking for another job. She couldn't keep up with the new hectic schedule, and well...*she* did have a personal life that was suffering.

Zora tuned it all out. As far as she was concerned, she worked hard so that she could fall into bed exhausted. Turned out her dreams had it in for her. All that would play during her deep slumber were memories of her and Jaxon. The first time they met, that crazy time in the ladies' bathroom and certainly that *Twilight Zone* first date. They were all great memories and more times than she cared to count, she would wake up with her pillow soaked with tears.

But all it took for those sweet memories to go

away was for her to remember his cruel words at his grandparents' estate or even how he'd looked as though he didn't know her.

"I should have told him," she admitted in the shower. Once the words were out of her mouth, the tears were down her face. She *knew* how Jaxon felt about his grandparents' needling. She should have broken her confidence with Melanie to tell the man that she loved the truth. But truth was a very tricky thing. Melanie just set her up on a blind date that technically never happened. But she knew none of that would matter to Jaxon.

He was stubborn, prideful and hardheaded.

And she loved him.

"I can't believe I'm about to say this," Dale said, sitting across from Jaxon in the Velvet Rope. "But, man, I hate to see you in here."

Jaxon rolled his eyes and pulled at his tie. "What? You're not having fun anymore?"

"How can I? Looking at your long face every night is dragging me down."

Jaxon shrugged as he waved at a new girl to bring him another drink. "I don't hear anybody else complaining."

"That's because you're shoving a lot of money down their G-strings, trying to get over Zora."

Jaxon glared at his friend. "I told you not to mention her."

"Yeah, well. My doctor told me to stop drinking, but I don't listen to him, either."

Jaxon received his fresh drink and tossed back half its contents before the waitress left the table.

"You love the woman. What difference does it make how you met her?"

"It makes a *big* difference. It means that this whole time everyone was playing around with *my* life." He shook his head. "You know I'd expected that sort of thing from Carlton, but from Grans? It means I just can't trust them."

"Oh, cut me a break." Dale rolled his eyes. "It's not like you're not above manipulating people, too. What about that whole fake fiancée thing—or the fact that you tried to blackmail the woman into going out with you—or fake a limousine to break down on the side of the road just so you could see whether she was going to be one of those high main-tenance chicks."

Jaxon shifted in his chair.

"So don't give *me* that holier-than-thou routine. You pull the same kind of tricks that your grand-father does. Why? Because you two are so much alike that you can't even see it. Your grandmother hired a professional matchmaker because she feared that you were about to make one of the biggest mis-takes of your life. News flash, that's what parents do. They look out for your best interests—whether you want them to or not."

Jaxon sat stubbornly in his chair. He didn't like the mirror Dale was holding up to him.

"He's right, you know," Kitty said.

Jaxon glanced over his shoulder at the smiling stripper in a sharp, black pantsuit.

Dale shook his head. "You don't have to take my word for it, Kit, but I don't think you're going to make good tips in that outfit."

"Shut up, Dale. It's my day off. I just came in to look at my schedule." She turned her attention to Jaxon. "As much as it pains me to say it, you should go after her. It was clear to me that first night you met her that there was an energy around you two. An energy that you cannot fake or manufacture."

Jaxon turned his head. "What—now you two are my therapists?"

"No. We're your friends. And friends do not let friends screw up their lives," Kitty said.

Dale set his drink down and pushed it aside. "Get out of here, man. You know you want her— so go get her."

"I just feel like this is all my fault," Sylvia croaked to Melanie and the Platinum Society staff. "I should have never put my nose where it doesn't belong. Now my baby isn't talking to me or to Zora. It's just one big mess."

"Shhh, now," Carlton said, curling an arm around his wife. "You know Jaxon. He just needs some time to calm down."

"Yeah, but he'll never forgive me."

Melanie felt horrible. When she glanced over at Vincent it was hard to not miss his I-told-you-so expression. "Everybody calm down. I'm sure that this whole thing will eventually blow over."

"I don't know," Sylvia said, shaking her head. "Jaxon can be stubborn. He gets it honestly from his grandfather's side of the family."

"Hey!" Carlton said, clearly affronted.

Sylvia patted his hand. "I'm sorry, baby, but it's true."

"Oh, I don't know." Jaxon's voice boomed into the office. "I think I might've gotten a touch of it from you, too, Grans."

Sylvia sprang to her feet. "Jaxon!" She rushed across the room and wrapped her arms around her big baby.

Carlton slowly rose to his feet as tears brightened his eyes. "Son?"

Jaxon glanced over and saw so many emotions coursing through the older man's face. "Hello, Carl—Grandfather."

A smile twitched up the corners of Carlton's lips, but he cleared his throat and said, "You made your grandmother cry."

"I know." He kissed the top of his grandmother's head. "I'm sorry about that. It won't happen again."

Carlton nodded. "See that you don't."

Sniffing, Sylvia pulled back and wiped at her

eyes. "What are you doing here? How did you know we would be here?"

"I didn't," he admitted and then swung his gaze toward Melanie. "Are you Ms. Harte? I went to Zora's apartment and I was told that she had moved. I guess I was sort of hoping that you could help me find my perfect match. I was hoping that you might know where I could find her."

Melanie's gaze shot over to Vincent, but now she was the one with the I-told-you-so smile before returning her attention to Jaxon. "You're in luck, Mr. Landon. Finding your perfect match is my business."

Chapter 25

Zora had always heard that the Cayman Islands were a great place to just get away. More now than ever, that was exactly what she needed. Her superwoman routine had finally caught up with her and she realized that she was on the verge of an emotional breakdown. When she had started crying in the shower that one morning, she found it damn near impossible to stop.

The plain and simple truth was that she missed Jaxon—terribly. Now that she had been able to admit that she did play a part in destroying a hard-earned trust that he'd given her. But where did she go with that knowledge? What was the next step since every part of her wanted him back and he wanted nothing to do with her?

But why is it so easy for him to walk away when it was just tearing her apart?

Evening after evening, Zora walked along the beach, ignoring the beauty that surrounded her. All she could do was think, wish and dream.

But she couldn't hide forever. It was time to return stateside. This time she was heading to California. Maybe being on the West Coast she could avoid so many memories that haunted her in New York. When she walked back into her bungalow, mentally preparing herself to start packing, she looked up and saw that she wasn't alone.

"Jaxon."

Standing in the room in white slacks and a sheer, gauzy white shirt, Jaxon gave her a nervous smile. "Hello, beautiful."

Zora didn't move for several heartbeats. She didn't know whether she could trust her vision or her hearing. But when the mirage didn't disappear, she reminded herself to start breathing. "What—?"

"Before you say something, can I speak?" he asked.

Zora pressed a hand against her chest as if that would stop her heart from trying to burst out of her chest. "Okay," she croaked, hearing that damn frog in her voice again.

"I love you," he announced.

Zora's knees nearly went out from under her.

"I've never stopped loving you," he added.

"When I look back on what happened that day at my grandparents, I *know* I overreacted. I think the whole thing just caught me off guard and it… brought up so many old feelings that…I just lashed out." He started moving toward her. "But these past months living without you has damn near driven me insane. I can't eat. I can't sleep. I can't stop thinking about you. You're in my head, in my dreams and in my heart." He stopped in front of her, reached out and caressed her face. "I know that I don't deserve it. But will you please consider—" he reached into his pocket and pulled out a Cartier box "—giving us a second chance?"

Zora stared up into Jaxon's black eyes that were glossed with tears. She could easily lash out and vent all the frustrations that she'd felt during the last few months, but suddenly those feelings had disappeared. All she felt at this moment in time was love. And she was not so foolish to risk throwing that away.

Tears leaked from her own eyes as she glanced back down at the ring.

"Please say something," Jaxon said, his usual deep baritone trembled.

She smiled and said the only thing she could say. "Absolutely."

* * * * *

REQUEST YOUR FREE BOOKS!

2 FREE NOVELS PLUS 2 FREE GIFTS!

KIMANI™ ROMANCE

Love's ultimate destination!

KROM10R

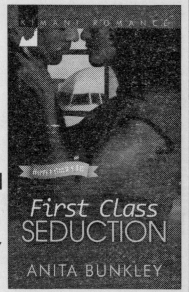